Echoes
from the
Alum Chine

Echoes
from the
Alum Chine

CYNTHIA STRAUFF

ISBN: 978-1-4834-6682-8 (sc)
ISBN: 978-1-4834-6683-5 (e)

Library of Congress Control Number: 2017903679

Lulu Publishing Services rev. date: 3/15/2017

for all the Lillian Gish Corporals
of the world …

Hollins Street

Helen Aylesforth, matriarch who was born and has lived all her life in this house

The Alley, Hollins Street

Myrtle Amos, lives behind the Aylesforth's home; works for Helen
Arbutus Corporal, daughter of Myrtle, wife of Randolph
Randolph Corporal, stevedore, husband of Arbutus
Christopher Columbus Corporal, known as Wanderer, son of Arbutus and Randolph
Lillian Gish Corporal, daughter of Arbutus and Randolph
Camelia Amos, daughter of Myrtle

Calvert Street

Cantata Aylesforth Sherwood, wife of Nicolas, daughter of Helen
Nicholas Sherwood, husband of Cantata, son of Charles Sherwood
Meg, servant

Park Avenue

Charles Sherwood, founder and president of Chesapeake Casualty Insurance Company
Alice Sherwood, his wife
George Hayes, chauffeur

St. Paul Place, Chesapeake Casualty Company

Violet Marsh, secretary
Edward Johnston, accountant
Mabel, switchboard operator

Ensor Street

John Abbott, cabdriver

My name is Lillian Gish Corporal, and yes, I was named after the actress. Blame my mother. I started out in life as Rose. My grandmother named me. Then my mother read about Lillian Gish. She would be a star, she said, and it would be a good thing for me to have that name. And what Mama says, happens.

Now, this is not my story, but I saw it. Rather, I saw some of it. What follows is what I remember, or think I remember, or what could have happened. It is not the whole story. What I didn't see, I made up. It's most likely as true as the rest.

PART I
New Year's Eve, 1912

Hollins Street

"I like the grey days." She turned from the window. "A proper way to start the year. Time for contemplation."

Helen Aylesforth looked over the cake that Myrtle had brought up from the kitchen. "No need to slice it now. I'll do that when Cantata arrives. Nicholas can make the drinks. The children won't eat anything except the chocolates. Just cover the plate; they'll keep." Helen waved her hand over the iced fruitcake that Myrtle had made the week before Thanksgiving, one that she herself had doused in bourbon every other day. She sat at the head of the table, stiff-spined, studying her folded hands.

Without raising her head, she said, "You just go on home, Myrtle. Enjoy the rest of your day."

Myrtle watched as her employer raised the thin china cup, using both hands, fingers that grasped it now so thin that the diamond-encrusted rings slid round so that the stones didn't show.

"Now, Myrtle, do not forget to send Randolph to call tomorrow morning. I'll be up. Remind him to come to the *front* door. A black-haired man as the first visitor." Helen smiled, patted the seat of the chair beside her, a signal for Myrtle to sit with her. "How long have we been doing that, Myrtle?"

Myrtle sat, filled her own cup, and, using the silver tongs, added three lumps of sugar.

"Ever since I can remember, Miss Helen, before you even married Dr. James. Your mama and papa always had a black-haired man come in

1

first. For good luck. Now we have Randolph go out and come back in our house too. Never pass up a time for good luck."

"Lots of years for us," Helen said. "And lots more ahead of us, God willing." Helen Aylesforth placed her hands in her lap, looked down into her cup. "Maybe not so good a wish, for too many years. Perhaps a wish for good ones, and be content with a few."

Myrtle, used to her employer's musings, most times melancholy, did not respond.

Helen Aylesforth rose and returned to the window, studying the yard, seeing the house where Myrtle had lived since they were both children. "And send Wanderer and Lillian over tomorrow afternoon, late. They can have the rest of the cake. I'll keep the tree up until Epiphany, but no more company for me, no more entertaining for a long while. I want a nice, quiet, grey January."

She turned, clasped her hands at her waist. "Now, is Wanderer enjoying his books?" Even she referred to Myrtle's grandson as Wanderer.

Myrtle answered, "Oh, yes. He's quite the reader."

"And Lillian? How is she getting along?"

"Well, Lillian Gish is not much of a talker. We're hoping that she comes out of herself more. She's only happy with Camelia. Those be two of a kind, I think. She's a shy one. Seems like Wanderer got all the personality in the family. Takes after his father, that one."

"Now you tell Arbutus to bring the child by some afternoon. I'll read to her. That might bring her around. Books."

"I'll tell her. But Lillian Gish, she most likes to stay with Melie."

"Now we cannot have that. No, that will not do at all. We must see that she develops herself. We must make her strong so she can make her way in this world."

Myrtle, sure that her employer couldn't see her, shook her head. Always making sure everybody is workin' hard, she thought, always taking charge for other people, sure she knows best, no matter who they are or what they might want for themselves.

She stood to clear the plates from the table, scraped the crumbs into the silver tray. Heading toward the stairs at the back of the house, Myrtle said, "I'll say goodbye now, Miss Helen. And you have a happy new year. Give my wishes to Miss Cantata and Mr. Sherwood. 'Butus thanks her for giving her so much work. Seems like she's sewing all the time now. And for Miss Cantata's friends too. All different dresses, so no one will look alike."

Helen Aylesforth walked to her. "Your daughter has a gift, Myrtle. I've been thinking about that as well. Of course, she can use the second-floor room for her sewing anytime she wants. But she can do more than just sew for Cantata and a few friends. Arbutus has a gift, and we are remiss if we allow that to lie fallow. Let us give thought to that in the coming year. Yes, we will work on that.

"Would it not be something if she had a shop, a shop of her own, maybe even employ other women. She could do that, Myrtle. Yes, certainly she could. I'll work on that, be thinking of that. This coming year."

Myrtle stopped, put the dishes on the sideboard. "Miss Helen, you are always working on something. Ever since I knowed you, you always hatching an egg."

★★★

St. Paul Place

Mabel pulled her headset off with a shake of her head, and replaced the seven plugs in their holders. No more calls today, she thought. New Year's Eve afternoon. No one will be working past 3 p.m. She put her hand to her hair, secured the strands that had fallen against the nape of her neck. Time to get home and brush some powder into it before Albert arrives, she thought. Perhaps that proposal I waited for on Christmas will present itself.

Nicholas Sherwood poked his head into her cubicle. "Almost time to close up shop for the day, or for the year, I should say." Mabel smiled and nodded. The younger Mr. Sherwood was trying to be nice, she knew, trying to make sure that the staff felt appreciated, but she didn't care about that as much as being able to leave on time every evening. The elder Mr. Sherwood always saw to that.

She walked to the office lobby where Violet Marsh was putting on her coat to leave. "All finished?" Mabel asked.

"Yes, typing done, filing completed for the year. Mr. Johnston is staying while they make sure that the numbers match so that they can close out the books for the year." Violet paused, debating whether to include a switchboard operator in on her thoughts. "Actually, it could wait, but you know Mr. Sherwood, senior. Such a stickler for accuracy, and 'honesty in business' as he calls it. If the papers are dated December 31, then, for him, the work should be done on December 31, whether or not his employees have better things to do."

Mabel laughed, and felt flattered that her coworker would confide in her like that. Maybe we can be friends, she thought. That would be nice. To have a friend in the office, one that I can call by a first name. And think of the gossip I can share with Violet, I who monitor, and sometimes listen in on, the calls that come to Chesapeake Casualty Company.

Her thoughts were interrupted as Charles Sherwood entered the anteroom, dressed, as he was every day, in his black frock coat.

"Wishing you girls a very happy new year. You have been a great help to us, making the wheels run smoothly." He extended his hand to both, though first to Violet.

Both women smiled; one wished him for her father. "And a Happy New Year to you as well, Mr. Sherwood," Mabel said. "Do you have plans for the evening?"

The older man raised an eyebrow. An impertinence, he thought, and then caught himself. New times, he remembered. Not everyone knew his, or in this case, her, place. Not her fault. A lack of upbringing, he decided.

"You enjoy yourselves, and we will see you on Thursday." He bowed and left the room.

Mabel turned to her new friend. "Yes, you enjoy yourselves," she mimicked with a giggle. Violet did not respond.

The elder Sherwood returned to his office where his son and his clerk, Edward Johnston, stood. "All in order here?" he asked, addressing his question to Johnston. Both men nodded their heads; neither spoke.

"Fine, fine. So, a good afternoon to you both. I'll go over your reports. No need for you to stay. I can call you if there is a problem. You both go on. Enjoy your holiday." He looked over at his son. "Nicholas, I will see you tomorrow."

Charles Sherwood unbuttoned his coat, moved to his chair, and flipped open the file.

The two men left the room. Nicholas turned to Johnston. "Don't worry. I'll see that it's fixed by week's end."

***

Park Avenue

As the car stopped at 604 Park Avenue, Charles Sherwood leaned forward to speak to his chauffeur. "You take this evening and tomorrow off, be with your family. Mrs. Sherwood and I are in until Thursday. We celebrate each year more and more quietly. Just so there is enough sherry for her, and enough bourbon for me." Sherwood laughed at his own joke.

George Hayes didn't realize that Sherwood meant his comment to be humorous. "Yes, Mr. Sherwood. Thank you. And may I wish you a Happy New Year, sir." Hayes moved to open the car's back door for his employer.

Sherwood waved his right hand. "No need, George, no need. I can get myself out. You just go along. My best to your family."

Hayes touched his hand to the brim of his cap, watched as his employer mounted the marble steps to his home. The front door opened as his foot touched the fourth, the top one. Mrs. Sherwood must have been waiting at the window, Hayes thought. He put the car into gear and headed north.

***

Calvert Street

Cantata Aylesforth Sherwood stood in the middle of her front room, surveying the newly upholstered sofa and chairs. Aqua, mauve, red-orange, violet, just like *Scheherazade*, she thought. Yes, people will be impressed. And if they don't recognize it, I'll just indicate the jacket of the phonograph record by the gramophone. Or, perhaps not point it out, but simply stand by it and be surprised when my hand touches it accidentally.

"Oh my," she rehearsed. "Look at this. *Scheherazade*. Such a stir it caused. Do you know it?" And, she decided, if they didn't see the parallels

5

between the costumes of the *Ballets Russe* and her new furnishings, then they were just not worthy of her efforts.

She turned when she heard Nicholas enter the room.

"Surveying your spoils?" he asked, his smile softening his words.

"Oh, I do love it. It is 'just the ticket,' as they say." She moved toward the stairway. "And we have no time to spare if we are to get to our table before the hors d'oeuvres have been whisked away."

An hour later Nicholas stood at the entryway, attired in comfortable, but fraying, white tie and tails. He called to his wife. "I'll bring the car to the front. You wait in the vestibule for me." She came to the head of the stairs. "Did you say goodnight to the children? They're with Meg, in the kitchen."

Cantata would have preferred to be driven by her father-in-law's chauffeur, but she knew better than to argue. Progress, her husband said, though she didn't always agree.

She descended the front stairway, lifting her hobble skirt to better manage the stairs. Arbutus has outdone herself, she thought. The women are certain to be jealous. She gave no thought to what the men might think. She called a goodnight down the back stairway, and heard her children respond. Meg would see that they had ice cream, a special treat, before she put them to bed.

Nicholas watched his wife. We do make a handsome couple, he thought.

They descended the steps to the street where the car waited. He opened the door for her as she slid onto the front seat of the white Oldsmobile, and, pulling two forest green-and-black wool blankets from the back seat, tucked them in around her.

"I don't know why we couldn't have asked for your father's car. It's covered, and Hayes could have driven us. We wouldn't have to arrive at The Maryland Club like two frozen sticks," she complained, and flounced as she pulled the ermine collar of her black-and-gold brocade coat around her, thrusting her hands up the fur-banded sleeves for emphasis.

Nicholas leaned over to her. "I haven't even seen your dress, yet,"

She didn't answer. She was thinking of how she would make her entrance.

★★★

The Docks

Randolph pulled his coat tight around him, wound the cashmere scarf (it had been Dr. Aylesforth's before he died) around his neck. It was soft, warm, and Randolph had pleated it carefully so that the hole from the cigarette burn didn't show at all. The wind from the harbor blew fierce, but he was smiling as he turned west, a walk that would take him home, toward his wife and children, and Myrtle and Camelia. He lifted his arm in farewell to his fellow stevedores, each on their own way home from the docks, stomachs still warm from their celebration.

A fine way to start the last evening of the year, Randolph thought, a bit of New Year's Eve festivity. Earlier in the afternoon, the men had gathered around the fires in the metal trash bins, rolled a few dice, enough to give Randolph a pocket heavy with change, though not heavy enough to leave any of the men ruined. The company supplied the spirits. Nice touch, Randolph decided. And the men shared the special treats their wives and mothers had included in their lunch pails that morning-- pickles, hard boiled eggs, even a coconut cake.

The crew chief had passed a pint of whiskey to each of them as they left for the day, this in addition to the bottles they had enjoyed that day. Just the way to start a holiday, Randolph decided, his fingers scampering up his sleeve. He practiced the fingering for his banjo, deciding on the songs he would play that night. Arbutus's favorites – *Bring Back My Lena*, though Randolph sang "Butus," not Lena. He smiled as he pictured her swaying as he sang *Every Little Movement*. He enjoyed that slow, tempered strum. So did she. Sometimes he whispered it to her at night, softly, when it was just the two of them, quiet. Then, for Myrtle, *Down by the Old Mill Stream*, and maybe a spiritual or two. That would please her. His mother-in-law always liked her spirituals. "You got a God-fearin' voice, even though you ain't a God-fearin' man," she would tell him, every time.

Randolph respected Myrtle. He was grateful for the house she provided for his family, and never forgot that it was she, through the intercession of Mrs. Aylesforth, who got him his job at the docks, a steady-enough job, a good-enough job.

As he turned the corner, Randolph thought about the year the world was leaving behind. Not such a bad one for him, his family. Enough food, a roof over his head, enough walkin'-around money. Not too many losses at the games, no, not too many at all. And then there was Arbutus, always Arbutus.

He whistled through his teeth as he turned the corner onto Mount Street. He knew Myrtle would have black-eye peas simmering on the stove. Always, she said, black-eye peas on New Year's. For luck.

"Joshua tol' me about them, said it was a necessity, so I did it then, and I'm doing it now. Colored folk need all the luck comin', and I'm not takin' a chance."

He inhaled deeply, smells of hams baking, sweet, sugary scents. People getting ready to revel. He and Arbutus would celebrate that night, early, and then he would find the game, just men for these games. He jingled the coins in his pocket. There'll be paper, yes, paper money, before January comes, he thought. Luck is with me, even before those black-eye peas.

Just before he reached Hollins Street, two miles into his journey, Randolph turned left into the alley behind the tall red brick houses. Smoke, a grey darker than the late afternoon sky, poured from the chimneys of the small wood cottages that stood on the unpaved dirt street, its inhabitants, most of them servants in the three-story houses that fronted on the Square, taking an hour for themselves before they were expected to return to their employers to complete preparations for festivities there.

Randolph knew that Myrtle would be finished her work for the day, that Arbutus would have stopped in to see if any final touches were needed. He was certain that Mrs. Aylesforth would send Arbutus home with enough meat and sweets to round out their own table.

A kerosene lamp in the window greeted him. It was Arbutus's way of saying welcome home. If she wasn't there, he knew that she was at the big house and would soon arrive, usually carrying a basket – of food, of fabric, of books for Wanderer.

He opened the door and the warmth of the house blanketed him. Myrtle, standing at the woodstove, turned when he entered.

"Ah, Miss Myrtle, smells good, feels good, in here." Camelia laid her knitting in her lap and looked in his direction. "I don't have to see you. You surely smell like you been celebratin' early, Randolph."

"That I have, sister, that I have. And I expect we'll be celebratin' through the night."

His mother-in-law turned to face the stove. "Not me. Not First Watch. I intend to be snug in the bed. Let the new year wash over me while I sleep. Me and Camelia." She looked down at the child. "And you too, baby. Am I right, Lillian Gish?"

The child nodded silently, and sidled closer to Camelia, pushing her thumb further into her mouth.

Wanderer looked up from his book. "I'll celebrate with you, Pops. Can we go out, downtown, maybe hear some music?"

Myrtle slapped down her spoon, and turned to him. "You better not let your mother hear you talk like that, boy. She'll take those books away from you before you can turn a page. The only music you'll be hearing tonight is in this house. Ain't I right, Randolph? You'll play for us, then we'll have an early night. Pray to Jesus to bring in a good year while we're all safe, all asleep. In this house. Maybe music be everybody snorin'." She gave a long look to Randolph as she uttered her last sentences.

Randolph put his arms around her. "Oh, Miss Myrtle, you keep us all on the straight and narrow. Don't nobody here need to worry about that."

Myrtle turned back to the stove, hoping to hide her smile.

Randolph hung his coat on a peg on the door, then walked to the side of the front room to sit on the bed that he and Arbutus shared. "Takin' off these cold shoes." He looked over at Camelia. "These socks you made do a good job, Melie, but that walk home, the chill comes up from the sidewalk all the way to my knees." He opened his arms to his daughter. "Come over here, my Lillian Gish, and warm up these old toes."

The girl smiled and pushed closer to Camelia.

"Okay, not today. That's okay, little girl," Randolph said.

He worried about that one sometimes. Not tonight, though. Not tonight. Randolph had plans.

Dinner eaten, songs sung, four of the family in bed in the back room, Randolph thought the time right to talk to Arbutus.

It was, and it wasn't.

"Don't you go there, Randolph. Don't you dare go there." Arbutus stood erect, moved close enough to stand toe to toe with her husband. She knew that the shoes she wore, ones that once belonged to Cantata until she had developed a bunion, placed her a full two inches taller than Randolph. Two inches. Not much perhaps, but she knew that it gave her an advantage that was not always present.

She thrust back her shoulders. "Don't think that I don't know where you're headed. Evangeline's son saw you there Saturday night, said you were winning, heard you tell them you'd be back on Tuesday."

Randolph waited until she took a breath, then reached out to touch her cheek.

"It's not what you think, 'Butus. I just go and watch, maybe put a few cents in, just extra cents. I don't get down there close. That's nasty, way too nasty for me. Just to have a little fun, hang around, you know. Just hang around." He took her hand and rubbed it against his cheek. "Then I come home to you. Always home to you."

Arbutus pulled her hand away. "Don't even walk past that doorway. There'll be no 'home to me,' if you go to that cock fight. You know that's trouble, troublin' men mixed up with that, no matter how far you stand back. And you want Wanderer to see that? You want him to think that's how we live? You want him to grow up thinking that's how to live?"

"Aw, 'Butus, you know you carryin' on about this. Just an hour, I promise. No lying. I tell you the truth. One hour. I'll be back. And you let me closer than the doorstep." He didn't correct her about just what kind of fight it would be.

Arbutus's arms were crossed. Randolph stroked the fingers of her left hand and grinned. He could see in his wife's eyes that he had won her over, again. He knew that his smile worked, most of the time at least.

Arbutus arms remained folded. "One hour. Then no more. You promise, Randolph. I don't want Wanderer to even know about that life, those people. You promise, Randolph, if you want to come closer than the doorstep."

"How about two hours, darlin'?"

Randolph checked the mirror to make sure his hat dipped to the right, just brushing his eyebrow.

Arbutus stood behind him. "Two hours. And you'd better come home with your watch. I mean it, Randolph. Two hours. You're a family man, not a gambler. You be careful what you teach Wanderer about being a man."

Randolph turned, put his arms around his wife. "We two men, in this house full of women, all telling us what to do. Need a little space, 'Butus, a little space, to be a man."

He twirled around, smiled, pulled on the brim of his hat. "But you know I'll be comin' home to you. You know that, baby." Touching his fingers to his lips, Randolph bowed and backed out of the house. Arbutus came to the door as he closed it.

"Two hours, Randolph. I mean it."

"Oh yes, my woman. Two hours. Be ready for me."

"I'll check that you have that watch before anybody's ready for anybody." She stopped herself from wagging her finger. "Be careful. Promise you'll be careful."

Randolph closed the door, smiling all the while.

Arbutus turned, walked to the doorway of the back room. Myrtle and Camelia were already asleep, Lillian Gish snuggled between them.

Must start making her sleep in the trundle, Arbutus thought. Get her used to being on her own, not so much a baby. Get her ready to grow up.

In the corner of the room she spied Wanderer, blankets thrown over what he thought was hidden. Arbutus knew. A flashlight and a book. She stood in the doorway, spoke softly so not to disturb her mother and sister. "Wanderer, no need to hide that book. You can sleep late tomorrow. No school for a while. You just read whenever you want."

She paused. "Is that one of Mrs. Aylesforths's books?"

Wanderer nodded and held up the dark grey volume. *The Book of Knowledge*. Mrs. Aylesforth gave it to me. She said I could keep it. There are a whole lot of books like this. Starting with the 'A's.' She said when I finish this one, she'd give me the next, and then the next, and then the next. Until I have the whole set.

"Hard words, but I'm sounding them out. Mrs. Aylesforth said to circle them – that I could write right in the book! And ask you about them, what they mean. I've got four so far. You want to know what they are?"

"Shush, Wanderer. Keep your voice down. Keep circling. We'll go over them tomorrow."

Arbutus looked over at him. Twelve years old, as smart as they come, she thought. Randolph's looks, and his personality. What a future in front of him. Going to school, reading, writing, doing cyphers.

Engrossed in this book, Wanderer had already forgotten her presence. She closed her eyes. Keep him away from Randolph's gambling ways. I need to pray for that, she thought.

Randolph, true to his word, arrived back at the house two hours and fifteen minutes after he had left, though with neither paper or coin weighing in his pocket. Last time, he said to himself, last time. Nasty it was. Rats fighting with rats. I'm done with that. Those last words he said aloud, and stomped his feet.

He exhaled, saw his breath in the frigid night. Time enough to ring in the new year with Arbutus, he thought.

She had allowed him that extra quarter hour, and had the bed turned down when he arrived. He grabbed her and laughed as he kissed her behind the ear. "Get those fancy clothes off and let me show you how to ring in 1913." Arbutus went behind the lace screen, opened the purple Louis Sherry tin that Cantata had given her, and inserted the dutch cap, grateful to Mrs. Aylesforth for her advice and help in getting it. She wanted her time for sewing, for reading, not for babies. She breathed a prayer of thanksgiving, not for the first time, for her sister. It was Camelia who served as Lillian Gish's mother. Well, she thought, they both thrived on it. No, she thought again, all three of us, Camelia, Lillian Gish, and I thrive on this arrangement.

She slipped on her cotton nightgown and went to Randolph. The less he knew about her preparations, the better.

New Year's Day, 1913

The Alley, Hollins Street

Randolph put on trousers and a newly-ironed white cotton shirt, and left to use the outhouse. On his way, he picked up the honey bucket that had been placed on the front stoop.

When he returned, he saw Arbutus standing by the front window. He went to her, put his arms around her waist. "You are dressed up this morning, girl. Ready to celebrate some more? That's Miss Cantata's? She give it to you, or what?"

Arbutus raised her left eyebrow, touched the side of her nose. "Yes, she *gave* it to me. Said she had worn it enough last year, and since I was the one who made it, she thought it only right that I have first pick. First pick? What did she think I was going to say?

"So, today being a holiday, I am dressed for it." She twirled around, lifting the heavy green velvet skirt to show off the black *passementerie* she had sewn on, stitch by stitch. She made sure to show her ankles and shoes, the latter also Cantata's. She lifted her skirt a bit higher, this time for Randolph's benefit.

Taking two steps back, he spun around. "Ah, now that's got it. 'Butus." And they laughed as he raised her skirt to her knee, showcasing the black-striped silk stocking.

"The best Christmas gift you ever gave me. And I don't want to know how you got hold of them," she said.

Randolph knelt, took her foot in his hand, and kissed it.

"Now that's just like an English gentleman in a book," Wanderer, who had been standing in the corner watching, cried out.

13

"You just go back to your readin'. Don't you worry about your poor ol' mom and pops," Randolph answered.

Camelia walked toward her. "Just let me feel, 'Butus," she said, as she reached out to stroke the soft fabric. "Ah, soft as silk," she added.

Wanderer looked up from his book. "Soft as velvet, you mean, Melie."

"Well, you know where I'm headed," Randolph announced, putting on his hat and overcoat, and doing a fine two-step from the house to the yard. Mrs. Aylesforth, who had been watching from her back door, waved and made her way to the front door.

Twenty minutes later, Randolph returned, carrying a fifth of Hunter's Baltimore Rye, this from Mrs. Aylesforth. She counted on his being the first to cross the threshold in a new year, a black-haired man. For good luck, she said. Randolph had filled that role ever since he had married Arbutus, and the older woman always had a bottle waiting for him to take home. "For being the man of the house," she said.

Wanderer looked up from his book when he heard the door close. "Pops wears his hat just like Tom Swift. Look." He held up the dark brown rectangle, Swift's dapper image on the cover.

"Maybe your Tom Swift wears his hat like I do," Randolph replied. "That one of your library books?" he asked.

"No sir. This is *my* book, part of my *personal* library. Mrs. Aylesforth gave me a stack of books as part of my Christmas package. Remember? And Tom Swift, he's an inventor, he goes everywhere, anywhere he wants to. And there's a colored man too. He goes with him. Andrew Jackson Abraham Lincoln Sampson, but they call him Rad. Eradicate is somewhere in there, too. But Rad, well, he is smart. They don't always think so, but he is, so he gets ahead of some of them. He's like you, Pops. He gets around them."

Arbutus looked up. "Wanderer, you stop that right now. Your father is a hard worker; he goes to work every day. He's not interested in 'getting around' anybody, as you say.

"And don't you be friends with anybody who says they're 'getting around' anybody. Not safe, Wanderer. Not smart, either. You find boys who read. That's who you want to be friends with."

"'Butus, no lectures today. It's New Year's. We should be celebrating, not worrying about who's reading and who's getting around," Randolph said, as he circled his arms around his wife's waist.

"Enough of that," Myrtle called. "Biscuits and gravy. Come and get it."

She brought a bowl to the table. "Enough of dresses, enough of preaching. Everybody come to the table."

The family of six sat close as they ate. Biscuits, white gravy, strawberry preserves. "There's eggs in the basket if anybody wants one," Myrtle said, between bites.

Randolph turned toward Lillian Gish who was leaning against Camelia.

"No thumb, Lillian Gish. Touch the ribbon on your braid when you feel like putting your thumb in your mouth. Just pull on that ribbon every time." Randolph put his hand to his hair, pulled on it.

Solemn-eyed, she smiled and removed her thumb, then tugged on her braid.

"You do that, then you talk more. All that listening you do. Takin' everything in." Randolph pushed his plate aside. "Come to Pops, baby."

Lillian Gish's lips opened in a wide smile. Then she quickly remembered to pull her upper lip down over her teeth. She shook her head. She knew she wasn't pretty, that she had buck teeth. That's what the boys in the alley said. She decided then to keep her mouth closed, not to talk. Except when she was with Camelia. Melie's blind and she's soft, Lillian Gish thought. She thinks I'm pretty. She'll love me.

★★★

Calvert Street

Meg brought the children to the kitchen. The family would have breakfast there; Cantata had given the cook the day off. She stood at the stove, wooden spoon in hand.

"I'm cooking this morning," Cantata announced. Nicolas had accompanied her to the ground floor thirty minutes earlier, and had set the table for five. "Meg, I hope you haven't eaten yet," he said. "Join us before you have your day off. A day without children, that should be a treat for you."

Meg looked at her employer. "Well, a day off is good. But I'm always glad to get back to the children." She shepherded the younger to the table. Christopher, the older, had already slid into his seat. Both realized how special the day was, their mother in the kitchen, and cooking.

"We will start the new year off right!" Cantata said, still flush from her evening at the Maryland Club and the celebration she and Nicholas had when they arrived home. Both thought it an appropriate way to start the new year.

"Please make sure the children are dressed before you leave, Meg. Then you can be off," Cantata said, still facing the stove. She frowned as she stirred the white sauce, which had become glutinous.

Meg went to her. "Perhaps a bit more milk, Mrs. Sherwood."

Hoping to keep the mood light, Nicolas brought the glass bottle from the ice box.

Cantata, in a combination of thanks and irritation, nodded to both. The milk did help, she admitted to herself as she stirred the pot.

After a breakfast of creamed chipped beef on toast, the toast prepared by Meg, the five dispersed, each to their duties of the morning.

At noon, Nicolas went to the stairs and called the children into the front room. "Off for our holiday visits. Come down now." He left Cantata to bundle them up and went to the alley to bring the car around.

When they arrived at the Park Avenue address, Alice Sherwood stood at the door to greet them. The children clambered out of the car into the arms of their grandmother.

"You've both grown since Christmas Day!" she said as she kissed Christopher, who now came up to her chin. And she reached down to cup Helena's chin. "You are getting more beautiful each time I see you. Those eyeglasses make you look not only intelligent, but very interesting. Helena, this is something you must remember: it is much more important to appear interesting than beautiful."

Cantata heard these last words, and was both pleased and irritated by them. Why do I feel so out of sorts today, she asked herself. Then she remembered.

An hour later, the family returned to the car.

"Why does Grandmamma only have fruitcake? It's horrible,"

Christopher complained. "I hope Grandmother Helen will have some chocolate."

"Hot chocolate, chocolate candies, chocolate cake," Helena sang.

Cantata turned sharply. "Enough. Now that's just enough. Respect your elders. This day is not for you. Just be quiet."

Both children lowered their eyes and were silent. Neither looked at the other.

Nicolas reached over and put his hand over his wife's. "Let's not take it out on them, Cantata. Just try to have an enjoyable time. Don't take things so much to heart."

Cantata pulled her hand away. "You just don't understand. You think she's perfect. You weren't there. You don't know. Half the time I don't think you believe me. It's all *la grande* Helen Aylesforth."

"Not now," Nicolas said, concentrating on maneuvering the car around the streetcar tracks in the middle of the street. "Let's just get through the day. We only have to stay a few minutes."

Helen Aylesforth did have chocolate candies, and milk, and fruitcake. The children were happy and quiet. Their grandmother sent them to the second floor, to the room with all the books. The conversation on the first floor was stilted, all three wishing the visit to come to an end.

After an acceptable thirty minutes, Helen stood. "Thank you for coming on the New Year's Day. It is always good to have a family visit. I appreciate the time you took driving here. And the children seem to be doing as well as expected. I hope that they are keeping up with their studies. Christopher is old enough to go to boarding school now."

Nicolas stood up to kiss his mother-in-law. "Mrs. Aylesforth, thank you for having us today." He went to the stairway to call the children, who had left the books to search the bureau drawers in their grandmother's bedroom. They slammed the drawer shut when they heard their father's voice, stifling their giggles.

"Mother, as always, this has been lovely," Cantata said as Helen offered her cheek for a kiss.

"Yes, and you look lovely this afternoon, Cantata. That is one of Arbutus's designs, am I correct?"

Cantata stood motionless, then nodded. At this, Helen continued,

"She is quite talented. I am thinking that she could do more than she is doing, sewing for you and your friends. Yes, I am thinking about that."

Cantata closed her eyes. Always thinking, always helping. When will you ever have time for me?

The family was in the car when Helena said, "Grandmother Aylesforth smells just like you, Mama."

Cantata turned to the back seat. "What are you talking about?"

"She and you. You two smell just the same. Is it because she's your mother? Do I smell like you too? Or will I when I grow up?"

Nicholas smiled. "It's their perfume, Helena. They both wear the same perfume. And when you grow up, if you want to smell like your mother, you can wear it too."

Helena bounced in the back seat. "What is it, Mama. I want to write it down so I remember."

Cantata faced straight ahead. *"L'heure Bleu*, Helena. Guerlain's *L'heure Bleu."* And she wondered why she always chose that scent.

Christopher punched his sister's arm. "You're stupid," he said, and went back to reading his book.

Thursday, March 6, 1913

The Alley, Hollins Street

He'd been assigned to the *Alum Chine*, a new ship for him. Some kind of crazy name, he thought, but the vessel looked to be not so big, not so hard to manage loading. He was grateful for that. Someone said that it was going to Panama, to build a canal. Randolph hadn't asked what a canal was. He waited until he was home that evening and mentioned it at dinner.

"Loading dynamite for Panama, for the canal," he said, then looking at Arbutus, "Do you know anything about that?"

She did, and she told him about the design of the Frenchman, and how it would change the world, let ships get from the east to California without going around South America. Randolph didn't even try to remember the man's name, all those unpronounceable syllables.

Of course, he thought, she would know all about that. Arbutus and her books, her reading, her knowledge about things that didn't mean anything and she couldn't even put a meal on the table.

He caught Myrtle's eye, and his mother-in-law shook her head. "It's a good thing you can sew, Miss Spouting-Off," she said.

Arbutus smiled and raised her eyebrows. She was used to, and proud of, this kind of teasing. Randolph chimed in. "And she's the most beautiful Negress in Baltimore. I don't need no book to tell me that."

Myrtle put down her fork. "Tell me why they're sending that stuff down there. How come it's coming from here?"

"To blow big holes in the ground, enough to get ships through. Right, 'Butus? Explosives, dynamite. Big signs on all of the packages. Danger most likely. But we don't have to worry. They said it's only dangerous if

19

someone lights one, or something like that. Nobody is allowed to smoke on the ship, so I ain't worried. It's just another job, nobody doing anything special."

Randolph reached in his pocket and handed Wanderer a rectangular object wrapped in brown paper, tied with twine.

Arbutus saw him. "What are you giving that boy now?" she asked.

Randolph patted Wanderer on the head as the child tore open his gift. "Take it on over in the corner. I'll show you how it works in a few minutes."

Myrtle stood. "It's a harmonica, ain't it? A harmonica." She turned to her daughter. "Arbutus, your father played one. Do you remember? Oh, too young, maybe."

She called to the bedroom where Camelia sat, rocking Lillian Gish. "Melie, do you remember Papa and his harmonica? Randolph's bought one home to Wanderer. Oh, Laws, we'll have the best music now. Banjo, harmonica. Melie, Arbutus, it will be like the old days. Just like Joshua back here with us."

Myrtle put her hand to her mouth, patted it. "Just like the old days."

Arbutus didn't smile. "Where did you get that?" she pressed her lips together. She fixed her eyes on Randolph.

Randolph folded his hands, placed them to the left of his plate. Assuming what he thought was the pose of Pastor Theodore, he intoned, "My dear Arbutus. You ask about the origins of this harmonica? I will tell you. Your earnest husband and father of Christopher Columbus Corporal, known to all as Wanderer, on his way home from a rigorous day at the docks, just happened to pass an establishment adorned with a sign of three balls hanging in front. If I understand correctly, such establishments cater to those who may be in temporary fiduciary distress, may need a dollar or two to tide them over until better times come along.

"As I walked by such establishment, a sparkle of silver caught my eye. I was led by the Lord, yes, by the Lord, to enter, whereupon I realized that said shining object was a harmonica, and a voice, yes, I do think it was the voice of the Lord, shouted, yes I say, shouted, not whispered, that Wanderer needed said object, that said object would bring pleasure not only to Wanderer, but to this entire household.

"So, I heeded the Lord's voice, and here I am."

Myrtle laughed through his entire speech. "Oh, Randolph, how you blaspheme!" she said between hoots. "We will be punished for sure. Pastor Theodore will box your ears in public for this."

Even Arbutus smiled and shook her head at her husband who could always turn a problem into a laugh,

"Now Randolph," she said, working to make her expression severe. "How did you get it?"

Randolph stood and walked to where his wife sat. He leaned down and rubbed his cheek against hers. "Don't worry, Arbutus, my beautiful one. I paid for it. I didn't pawn anything. I paid for it. Twenty-five cents, cash on the barrelhead. Nothing, not a thing to worry about. Only dream of the music Wanderer will make."

Arbutus turned, folded her arms. "And just where did you get that twenty-five cents, 'cash on the barrelhead'?"

Randolph took her hands in his, unfolded her arms. "You leave the worrying about that to me."

"You are incorrigible," she answered, and walked to the back of the house.

Randolph looked at Myrtle. "Incorrigible. Did you hear that? That must mean handsome."

Myrtle smiled and shook her head. "And it's a good thing that you are."

March 7, 1913

The Alley, Hollins Street

Randolph heard the alarm clock and reached over to turn it off. Arbutus rolled over and pulled the blanket over her face. He patted her head as he sat up to pull on his gray flannel work shirt and denim trousers. He had slept in his socks.

All in the house were asleep. He looked over at his wife. Arbutus slept with the sheet and blanket over her face. How could she breathe? he wondered. She told him it made her feel safe, protected.

"You don't need to worry," he'd tell her, and then pull the sheet away. She'd always laugh, roll over on her side. And, a minute later, the sheet would creep up until her head was completely covered.

Watching Arbutus, he thought of the first time he had seen her, dressed in velvet and lace, marching down Hollins Street like she had a right to live there. Arbutus, the prettiest one. He remembered. The prettiest one, a book in her hand when he met her. He should have known.

Wearing green velvet. She said it matched her eyes, told him that the very first day, almost the first thing she said to him, after he asked her where a beautiful green-eyed goddess was headed.

Where did she get green eyes anyway? And that dark brown skin, darker than mine. Randolph smiled at the memory.

He looked in at Wanderer, blankets in a heap on the floor despite the chill in the air. Randolph had yet to light the wood stove. Wanderer, what a name for my boy, Randolph thought. Christopher Columbus, I named him, but Myrtle has always called him Wanderer, and she's right. Walking before he was ten months old, afraid of nothing, always walking, looking, always searching. We should call you Curious, he whispered to his son. Lillian Gish, left thumb in her mouth, slept snug between Myrtle and Camelia.

Randolph knew that Arbutus wasn't cut out to be a mother, not a doting one at least, not like Myrtle. He wondered where his wife got her hardness, her stern outlook on life, a lot like Mrs. Aylesforth. Perhaps that was why the two got along so well. Just a good thing that Myrtle was there, and Camelia, though she could hardly see. Still, they kept the children safe, tended to.

Arbutus, with her sewing, and all that reading, like she had no time for her own children.

He had thought that Lillian Gish would grow up silly, flighty, for she had been, early on, interested only in the lace and beads and baubles that Arbutus brought home, castoffs from the Aylesforth women. Randolph looked over at his daughter, sleeping soundly, happily, he thought, between the two women she was sure who loved her. So quiet, turned in on herself she had become. He wondered about that.

He walked to the kitchen, shrugged into his brown wool coat, wrapped the plaid scarf around his neck, pulled his red-and-black knit cap, a Christmas present from Camelia, low over his eyes.

There was no sign of the sun as he stepped out into the early cold morning. The gas lights at the corner shed dim shadows on the alley. He carried the honey bucket to the outhouse. On his way back he brought two logs in from outside the door. The house would be warm when the rest of the family stirred after daybreak, he thought, as he shoved the wood in the stove.

Myrtle had left two biscuits for his breakfast. Randolph split one and laid thick country ham slices between the two halves. He wrapped up the second; he'd eat that when he got to the docks. At the stove he pulled his cup from the hook and poured in the syrupy black coffee that Myrtle had prepared the night before. He drank it cold; he'd developed a taste for it that way. He'd have two more cups of hot coffee once he arrived at the docks. Someone, Randolph never wondered who, always had it ready, and those tin cups kept his hands warm while he drank it. He took it black, could never understand those who added those heaping spoons of sugar and milk until it was almost white. That was how Arbutus drank hers.

Woman's drink, he thought, as he watched the men doctor theirs. Too much trouble, anyway. Yes, I'll have me real coffee at work, the kind you can smell a block away, not Miss Myrtle's concoction, more chicory than coffee beans.

Randolph picked up the metal lunch pail his mother-in-law had packed the night before. The standard fare, two sandwiches, one meat, one cheese, a slab of butter, a cookie or two if there were any left, a piece of cobbler wrapped in waxed paper, and a piece of chocolate. Myrtle said that Mrs. Aylesforth had declared that "it behooves a man to have a delicacy as part of every meal." A *lagniappe*, Myrtle called it, a word she learned from Joshua, from his Louisiana days, "just somethin' special, a nice surprise."

Randolph always put such things in his pocket, unwilling to let his coworkers see evidence of such foppery. Myrtle and Miss Helen. His mother-in-law thought her employer infallible. Still, Myrtle was a good cook. It occurred to him that she was the only cook. Arbutus couldn't be bothered; Camelia hadn't come near the stove, not since the fire so many years ago.

Arbutus had her sewing, and her books. Mrs. Aylesforth and that library card of hers. No thought of children or cooking. Good, good Miss Myrtle, Randolph thought. We'd be in a pickle without her.

In the damp, dark cold morning, he walked toward Pratt St. avoiding the patches of ice that would melt that day only to freeze again at sunset. He whistled *Waiting for the Robert E. Lee,* and pictured the movement of his fingers on the banjo. His feet moved to the syncopation of the ragtime songs. He thought of Wanderer, of teaching him to play the same songs on the new harmonica, saw the family gathered round, listening, laughing, clapping in time to the music. He pictured Arbutus and smiled, seeing those small even, white teeth flashing as she laughed, always showing the tip of her pink tongue, touching that sharp tooth to the right.

Oh, he had a prize in Arbutus, he knew that.

He closed his eyes and inhaled the acrid, sweet smell of the coal fires, signaling the start of the day. When he opened them, he saw the bus approaching. His workday had officially begun.

Twenty-five minutes later, as he turned the corner toward the wharf, a different odor came to him, stronger, smoke and rotting fruit, vegetables, sewerage, and brine. A not unpleasant smell, he thought.

A few of the men had gathered beside the pier, warming their hands around the fire set in the bin, drinking the first of many cups of coffee. Most had a flask, or a pint bottle, in their pockets, which they visited often. To get them through the day.

Randolph left John Barleycorn alone while he worked. Not good to overdo, he believed. Save it for the good times, save it for a higher quality liquor.

"A full day's work, looks like," one of the men said. The group looked over at the railroad siding where stacks of crates, taller than two men, the length of five railcars, waited.

Randolph spoke up. "For the canal. They'll be blasting for weeks. And as cold as it is here, that's how hot it is there. Like Hell, they say. Hell with bugs." He took a last gulp of coffee, threw the rest in the harbor.

He heard one of the stevedores call, "Don't nobody go lighting up today. Not anywhere near here." Another laughed as he tossed the remains of his coffee onto the ground. "If he does, it will be the last time. For him and for us."

The men were silent as they worked, moving the crates, stowing them in the holds of the ship. Three foremen ensured that the work developed its own music, efficient in its rhythm, equipment and men moving without stopping.

At ten a.m. the first foreman blew a whistle. "Take a rest. Ten minutes. Stay at your places."

Further down the line, the second foreman shouted. "Clear out this lot before you stop.

The third called to his crew. "Keep on loading. Looks like you can take a break at 10:30."

Randolph felt in his pocket for his cigar. He allowed himself one cigar a day, always on the morning smoke break.

★★★

St. Paul Place

Charles Sherwood felt it before he heard it, a deadened thud in his chest, his heart clenching, then a piercing shudder in his brain, his ears aching from the sound. A heart attack, he thought. Surely I am having a heart attack. Then silence. He heard, felt, his heart beat, realized that his fingers were clutched around his pen. As he willed himself to loosen his grip, Violet Marsh entered his office without knocking.

"A bomb, Mr. Sherwood. It has to be a bomb." She clutched her lined steno pad to her chest. "The anarchists, those anarchists, I'm sure. They're coming for us. They're coming. I know it. Those Russians, Italians, that man. You know who I mean. I can't think of his name. First those bombings in Chicago, now they're coming here."

Sherwood stood, steadied himself, cleared his throat, unsure that he could make his voice heard.

"Miss Marsh, we must remain calm. All is well here. The blast was close, yes, but it was not in this building. We can rely on the police to handle this. Let us remain—"

Before he could finish his sentence, his son rushed into the room.

"Father, did you feel that blast? The windows in my office shook. Do you suppose it was a bomb? An explosion somewhere? City Hall? Should we send someone out to find out?"

"Nicholas," Sherwood addressed his son sharply. "Let us be still for a moment. We don't want to send anyone out into danger. We must be sure that we are safe ourselves, that there are not more bombs set to explode." He returned to his chair, drew a fresh piece of company letterhead from the top left-hand drawer of his mahogany desk, dipped his pen into the inkwell.

"First, we will contact the police," he said as he wrote. "Let us find what they know, what they advise." He turned. "Miss Marsh, you sit, stay here with me. Nicolas, find the staff, tell them that we are in the process of discovering just what happened. Make sure they move to a safe place, away from any windows. You, go to the entrance, lock it. It would not be a bad idea to put some barricades up as well. See what you can do about that."

Sherwood picked up his phone, relieved that the connection hadn't been severed. "Mabel, good that you are still at the switchboard. Remain at your station. Don't worry. We're attempting to find out what happened. Meanwhile, connect me with Captain Blair at the Central Police station. I will speak only with Captain Blair. Make that clear when you call."

Less than three minutes later, Sherwood had his answer.

"An explosion apparently," Sherwood said as he replaced the earpiece. "Somewhere in the Patapsco River. That's all they know. Miss Marsh, you will inform the staff. Tell them that all is well here. Everyone is safe. No cause for worry. We will continue our workday as usual. Please see that that message is delivered."

He added as an afterthought, "And find the younger Mr. Sherwood. Tell him what I learned. Instruct him to remove any barricades he may have put into place. Tell him that I asked you to deliver that message."

As his secretary left his office he called to her. "Yes, and tell him to report to me right away."

The woman nodded, placed her pencil behind her left ear, and left the office, her notebook still close to her chest.

Sherwood replaced his pen, leaned back in his chair, rested his hand on his heart. Harbor explosion. He realized that it meant money, insurance payouts. And he wondered who and how much.

When his son appeared at his door, he beckoned him in. "Walk down to Pratt Street. Find out what you can. I don't want to bother the police. The explosion was apparently further to the south, so there should be no problem by this part of the harbor. Come back and let me know what you find. Listen to the gossip as well as the facts. There is bound to be cross-over.

"And stop at the Joyce and have them prepare lunch for you to bring here. Best for us to stay by the phones. Bring something for the switchboard girl as well. Make sure that she knows not leave her station, that it is an emergency. Let us hope that the damage is limited. No lives lost. But if the ship was anywhere near Fort Carroll, with such a massive explosion, I very much fear that it could have been the dynamite. If that is the case, we must be prepared, before we are contacted. Cottman, they will be in the soup. And we might just be in there with them."

***

Hollins Street

Myrtle walked the five blocks east that morning, one wicker basket tucked into the larger one. Helen Aylesforth ate little these days, but had given her a few ideas for the rest of the week. Myrtle needed to go to the market only on Wednesdays and Saturdays now. And though she was grateful for her lightened workload, she missed the company, and the gossip, of her friends. Not so many there anymore; the owners of the big houses dying, replaced by a new generation, with automobiles, electricity, phones. So much activity, so much change. Even her own children, all but Arbutus and Melie, scattered, on their own, making, she hoped, a new way in the world.

Myrtle liked staying where she was. It felt safe to her, working in the same house, the big house right where her parents worked. House slaves they were at first. Then the war. They stayed put, same house, behind the big house, facing the alley, she, assigned to tend Miss Helen as far back as she could remember. Now both of them old, widows, watching their children leave, one way or another.

Myrtle stopped at the corner of Carrollton and Hollins Streets, closed her eyes, thought of Joshua. Married him at fifteen. Married, done right, at St. John AME Church, right on Carrollton Street. Miss Helen and the family came, all of them. "Joshua," she said aloud, feeling still in love with that handsome, dark brown face, those bright eyes, those white teeth that sparkled when he smiled. An Arabber going up the street, down the alleys, wagon full of vegetables. Told me he saved the best for me. Perhaps, sometimes, he did. Myrtle smiled at the thought and pulled at the mole on her neck.

Miss Helen got him a job on the docks. Steady work, a more respectable profession, she said. When the children started coming, Miss Helen told her that she needed to be home with them until they could manage on their own. First John, as handsome as his father, always angry because he had to take care of the little ones, said it was "women's work." Until the fire. Camelia trying to heat water to surprise Myrtle with a cup of tea that afternoon. As blind as she was, they knew that she could see only shapes.

John saved the day. And he changed after that. Always looking over his shoulder. Not that it did any good.

Daisy, Leroy, died less than a year apart, less than a year old, both of them. Then John, run over by a train, run right over, so she never got to see his body, never held it to say goodbye to her boy. Joshua said it was best. He was my favorite. They all knew that, but I didn't care. They said he was drinking. Maybe so.

James and Solomon, they didn't want to stay in Baltimore, wanted adventure they said. James first, going to Philadelphia. Solomon, running away to join him. Disappeared, both of them. Watch over them, she prayed, sure that her words were heard.

"Thank you, God, for Camelia and Arbutus." She said these words aloud and thought of Arbutus, coming after all those years, when she thought she was done with birthing and all that went with it, years after Solomon was born. All those beautiful names of flowers, she thought. She and Joshua had agreed that she would name all the girls, he the boys. All flowers, just like her mother did. Such beautiful names, Poppy, her sister, Snapdragon, her mother. Dead. So many dead.

Well, where we all go, Myrtle thought. Best to concentrate on the living, she decided, and was surprised to see that she was already in front of the market. My feet delivered me while my mind was, well, my mind was with my thoughts. Not a bad place to be. This she didn't say aloud.

She nodded to the man behind the butcher stall and held her breath as she passed. Still, the odor of blood stung her nostrils. She reached into the pocket of her apron for her coin purse, leather, once belonging to Cantata.

Myrtle decided to start with the vegetables – four turnips, three parsnips. There were enough potatoes in the bin. Miss Helen could use a few cakes, Myrtle thought, and bought two from the confectioners, along with three muffins she'd take home for her own supper that night.

As she returned to the meat stall, she felt the ground shake. The lights shuddered as the gas jets flickered. Myrtle heard women scream, although she thought she herself was quiet. She leaned against the nearest stall to catch her breath. Apples spilled onto the floor, hitting her feet. Then all was quiet.

"A bomb. Everyone stay where you are." A man's voice, deep, author-itative. Thank God, she thought. Someone here to take charge, make things right, keep us safe. She felt someone grab her, yanking at her arm. She looked over to see Charlotte, whom she had known for years, Charlotte, who lived three houses up the alley. "We gotta get out of here. Into the street. Safer there. Don't wanta be inside with no bomb going off."

A small crowd gathered on Arlington Street, each speculating on what and where. A mounted policeman angled his horse into its midst. "Disperse. Go to your homes. Disperse."

Myrtle looked at his face and saw that he was as frightened as the rest of them, maybe worse because he was working so hard to look like he wasn't.

Those assembled backed away. "Do you know what happened? Was it a bomb? Was it here?" someone asked. Then, as one, heads turned toward the south, the sky now filled with plumes of thick black smoke. The harbor, looks like, Myrtle thought, then corrected herself. No, it's too far south.

She heard someone call to the policeman. He pulled his horse to the middle of the street. "They just told us to get people off the street. Didn't tell us nothing else."

Most of the customers had left the market. The vendors, grumbling, righted their wares and hoped that customers would return in the afternoon.

Charlotte still held Myrtle's arm. 'Come with me. I'll see you home. No trouble here. We're safe."

Myrtle breathed a sigh of relief. "I need to get some pork chops. I'll be home after that. Come by this afternoon. I have some extra muffins I can give you."

Charlotte left and Myrtle turned to return to the market. "We're all safe," she thought and breathed deeply. Then she remembered.

Randolph.

She turned and ran to the back of the big house, let herself in the back door, calling out as she ran to the front room. "Miss Helen, an explosion. Randolph, Miss Helen. We got to go to the docks."

Finding the room empty, Myrtle ran to the stairs, using the banister to pull herself up. "Miss Helen. An explosion." She opened the door to the front bedroom.

Helen had been lying atop the spread. Hearing Myrtle, she had raised herself up on her elbow. Her feet felt for her shoes.

"That noise a while ago, that was an explosion? It was at the docks? Not a bomb? Which dock? How do you know this?" Helen struggled to clear her mind of the fugue of sleep.

"Do you know where? Are you sure it's where Randolph is?" She sat up, erect. "Let us not panic. The docks are miles long, miles. And even if it were where Randolph is, he may not be harmed."

She cleared her throat, put her hands in her lap. "You know, Myrtle, when trouble strikes, the first thing one must do is keep calm, keep our wits about us so that we can think clearly."

She reached down to adjust her left shoe. "And we must be grateful that is wasn't a bomb."

She stood, held on to the bedpost until she was sure of her balance. "How do you know that it was an explosion? How did you learn that? Exactly who told you?"

Helen Aylesforth had regained her composure. She was now in charge. Both women recognized this and were grateful. She patted the bed, a signal for Myrtle to sit.

Helen looked down at Myrtle, took her hand. "Take a breath. Tell me, tell me what you know."

Myrtle knew that she must be calm. She struggled to collect herself, waited through the silence, finally spoke. "The police. They were by the market. We thought it was a bomb that hit the market. Everybody running every which way. The police came, made us leave, then tol' us we could go back in, or maybe they didn't say that. People saw the smoke. The police, they didn't know from nothing, no more than the rest of us.

"We saw the smoke. The docks, people said, or maybe they said the harbor. That's when I heard that it was an explosion, by the docks. Or the harbor. I can't think straight. Everyone was talkin' about it on the street, on the way home, everybody talkin' at once. When I remembered Randolph, that's when I ran here. I haven't even told Melie, or 'Butus. And 'Butus is with Miss Cantata today. I got to go to her too. And look for -"

Helen stopped her. "So you didn't hear this from a policeman, just on the street. So we are really not sure. Myrtle, let us pause, think, decide exactly what we should do, what we need to do." She hesitated, then continued. "Yes, let us think." She walked to the window, then turned, touched her right temple with her index finger.

"First, Arbutus is with Cantata. Let me call there. Or perhaps get in touch with Mr. Sherwood first. He is downtown. He would know facts. He would be the one to contact. We need to start there. We need facts, facts."

Myrtle put her hand to her chest. "You do that, Miss Helen. But I know it's trouble. I was born with the veil. It's Randolph. He's dead. I know it." Myrtle moved to the doorway.

"You know nothing of the kind, Myrtle. Let us keep our wits about us." Helen's tone was sharp. "First we will contact Mr. Sherwood. Yes. He will have knowledge. We must have facts before we act." Helen moved past Myrtle and led the way downstairs to the telephone table in the hallway. The phone rang as she walked toward it. She lifted the earpiece.

Without waiting for a greeting, Cantata spoke. "Mother, I just talked with Nicholas. An explosion at the docks. He was on his way there. And Arbutus has already left. She's going to Locust Point, though I'm not sure that's where the explosion was. I offered to call a cab for her, but she ran out of the house. Said she couldn't wait.

"I told her to wait until we had more details, but she wouldn't listen. She's left her bag here, didn't take it with her. I don't know how she will manage, don't know if she has any money with her at all.

"Perhaps -"

Helen interrupted her. "I'm here with Myrtle. I was just about to call Mr. Sherwood. We know about the explosion." Helen paused. "I will hang up now. I need to think about how to handle this." Helen replaced the earpiece without a goodbye.

Myrtle watched her employer, waited for her to make things right.

Helen turned. "Myrtle, you and I will go to Locust Point. That's where Arbutus has gone. She neglected to take her belongings. So she will need us. If all is well, we will have a relieved ride home. We still do not know the location of the explosion, or if anyone was hurt. Let us not jump to any conclusions.

"While I call a cab for us, you let Camelia know where we are. She needs to keep Wanderer and Lillian with her when they arrive home from school. If there is trouble, if we are not back home by then, make sure that she keeps them with her. We can't have Wanderer out on the street."

Myrtle found her older daughter, told her what to do. Camelia said that she would spend the time praying. "On my knees prayers. They go right to Jesus, right to him." She laid her crochet hook down beside her and put her head in her hands.

Myrtle went to the bedroom and brought in the Bible. "You do that, child. You do that. Pray for Randolph. Pray for all of us. I know he's dead. I feel it in my bones."

Camelia knelt with her Bible as Myrtle left the house.

Helen paced as they waited. "Go out on the step. You'll be able to see the cab coming. Then rap on the door. I'll be ready by the time it gets to the house."

When the cab arrived, Helen bundled Myrtle in before her. The driver raised an eyebrow, but after a look from Helen, offered Myrtle a blanket for her legs. When he returned to Helen, she said, "No time for that. Take us to the docks, Locust Point. We are in a hurry. We need to get to the explosion site."

"Then you don't want to go to Locust Point. I heard that the ship was near Curtis Bay."

"Oh Laws, now I know he's dead for sure." Myrtle pulled her handkerchief from her pocket, wiped her brow.

Helen ignored Myrtle, addressed the driver." How do you know the ship was there? How do you know that? How do you know that was the location?" Her tone was brusque.

Another rich old woman acting huffy, John Abbott thought, though he answered with a mustered politeness. "It's all the talk. Dynamite ship it was. Then a tug sunk. Dead. Everyone dead is what they are saying. No survivors."

Myrtle groaned and stared straight ahead. Helen reached for her hand, then cleared her throat, addressed the driver. "Rumors are always dire, are they not? Let us hope for the best. People always make more of things than they are. I am sure, in your line of work, you have found it thus."

Abbott shrugged and concentrated on maneuvering the cab through the congested streets. "You know, it's not easy getting there. I don't go there regular, don't think I've ever taken a fare there."

Then Helen remembered. Arbutus. Cantata had said that Arbutus was going to Locust Point. She tapped the driver on his shoulder.

"First we must go to Locust Point. Take us there right away, then we can go to Curtis Bay. Perhaps by then you will have your wits about you."

Abbott, swallowed, shook his head. Rich old woman, he thought. But he knew how to get to Locust Point. He turned the cab to face the east.

As he turned onto Ostend Street, Helen called for him to stop. Both she and Myrtle had seen Arbutus, standing alone, a tall figure with her head bent. Myrtle ran to her. "Oh, baby, we found you. Miss Helen is here. She's goin' to take us to Randolph. Everything will be all right, baby. Yes, it will," she said, though she knew her words were lies.

The three women crowded into the back seat of the cab. Abbott thought he knew the purpose of their journey, felt bad for the tall woman. She cut quite a figure, he noted.

"Now, take us to Curtis Bay," Helen commanded.

While Abbott drove, he tried to work out the best way to approach the area. He decided to take Pennington Avenue and hoped that by the time he reached its end he would be able to see the wharfs. He gripped the wheel as the cobblestones changed to gravel.

Two blocks before he reached the water, he was stopped by barricades. Police cars, ambulances, electric and horse-drawn, moved in what looked like random directions.

"This is as far as we can go, Ma'am. What would you like me to do?" Abbott turned to face Helen.

"For God's sake, man, you know the city. Find us a way that we can get closer. Side streets, you must know them all."

Abbott sighed. These society bitches, he thought, and then remembered Myrtle. Maybe not, he decided, and jerked the cab to the left, waved to a mounted patrolman as if he belonged, and, once he reached Birch Street, drove to within a block of the water. He turned toward the women in the back seat.

Before he could speak, Helen said, "No need to explain We will get out here. Thank you for your help this afternoon. I think we will be able to manage."

She handed the driver a dollar bill. "You may keep the change," she added, as he helped her from her seat. She stood, waiting for him to go to Myrtle's side. Abbott hesitated, and before he could reach her, Myrtle had left the cab and was hurrying toward the barricade.

"Wait. Myrtle, wait," Helen called, then faced the cab driver. "Thank you. You did an exemplary job. What is your name? I'd like to use you exclusively for my driver. To whom must I talk to arrange that?"

Abbott hesitated. He did not want to be stuck with this imperious woman any longer than this fare.

But he answered. "John Abbott, ma'am." And he wrote down the number of his cab and gave it to her.

Taking the paper, but not waiting for a response, Helen hurried toward Myrtle. Stopping her, she said, "We must think of how to move forward, must choose the best course of action. We must think, Myrtle, before we act."

★★★

The Wharf

The women threaded their way through the chaotic scene. Police attempted to control crowds of on-lookers, tried to keep reporters away from the scene, struggled to keep the area clear for the ambulances and their workers. The steamer had disappeared, as had the tugboat that had hurried to help it.

Helen, still holding Myrtle's hand, acknowledged the policemen with a polite nod. The three women then walked directly by them and the barricades.

Arbutus stepped aside to allow two stretcher-bearers past, then reached out to pull away the sheet that covered the body. Bloodied though the man was, it was not Randolph. The men attempted to step around her. She blocked their way. "Where are you taking the injured?"

"Ambulances taking the injured away; don't know which hospitals, different ones, most likely. Dead are laid out over there," one called, tossing his head to his right as he continued on his way.

Arbutus started to speak. Helen interrupted her. "Let us not talk now.

We must think, not run willy-nilly. Arbutus, you go toward where the ambulances have gathered. Myrtle and I will examine the deceased. Then we will meet back here, right at this spot. Regardless of what we find, and we must determine our next steps."

Arbutus, thankful to receive some direction, nodded and ran toward the street. Myrtle and Helen walked more slowly.

The three gathered a few minutes later. Arbutus searched Myrtle's face for a sign. "No Randolph," Myrtle said.

Arbutus pressed her hand to her mouth, struggled to maintain her composure. "Not dead," she whispered.

"No, not that we know," Helen responded. "Now, it appears that you did not find Randolph with the injured."

Arbutus inhaled deeply, knew that she must present a calm front to Mrs. Aylesforth. "No, all the ambulances had left by the time I got there. Some bystanders told me that the injured had been taken away, colored and white, that they were sent to different hospitals. They didn't know where." She hesitated, and her voice broke as she said, "We need to go; we need to find Randolph."

Helen Aylesforth looked at Arbutus, and was surprised to feel the sting of tears. She looked away as she spoke. "Arbutus, Myrtle, I have just realized that we are assuming the worst. It could be that Randolph was not injured at all, that he has returned home to tell everyone that he escaped injury, that he is unharmed. And here we are, all worrying, while he may be worrying about us. Yes, I am sure that is the case." She stood straight, still looking away from the harbor. "So, we will take a cab together and go home – to Randolph."

She pulled a paper from her purse. John Abbott, cab #7. She would remember that for the future.

When they arrived at the alley, Randolph was not at home. Helen stood with the women in the front room. Camelia helped Myrtle to the table, then went to the stove to heat water for tea. Arbutus moved to help her sister. Helen sat at the table. Arbutus scooped out the tea leaves, covered them with boiling water.

Myrtle sat quietly, looking down into her empty teacup. "He's dead. I know it. I knew it when I first heard of the explosion. All that blaspheming last night, making fun of the Lord, calling the Lord's wrath down upon him, upon all of us."

"Mama, that is crazy talk. Ain't no Lord botherin' about what Randolph said." Arbutus poured the dark brown liquid into the cups, then opened the door, looked up and down the alley. It was empty.

Helen spoke. "We need a man's wisdom here. To help us see what to do next. Let me call Mr. Sherwood, senior. He can advise us." She rose to leave. "Arbutus, perhaps you would care to come with me."

To Myrtle she said, "Myrtle, it is not good to be superstitious," and she and Arbutus left to go to the big house.

***

Hollins Street

Helen replaced the earpiece and turned to Arbutus, who had heard one end of the conversation.

"Mr. Sherwood, senior, has agreed to allow the younger Mr. Sherwood to escort me to the City Morgue. This is a most extraordinary occurrence, but in this case, I convinced him that it is necessary. It is best that I go, that you stay here with Myrtle and the children. They should have already arrived home from school.

"There is a slight possibility that Randolph is dead, and, Arbutus, I emphasize that it is slight. Please remember that. However, Mr. Sherwood and I decided that it is best if we first ascertain that, and then, if he is alive, which I believe to be the case, our next step will be to contact, or even visit, the hospitals that received the injured."

Arbutus remained where she stood.

"Are you taking this in, Arbutus?" Helen asked.

The younger woman nodded.

"Good. Mr. Sherwood should be here soon. Meanwhile, you go home. I will come directly to the alley when I return."

Helen reached out, took Arbutus's hand, then pulled her toward her, patted her back. "It will work out, child. Everything always does."

***

St. Paul Place

Charles Sherwood sat down at his desk, then stood and walked to the window. The *Alum Chine* at the bottom of the Patapsco River, sunk in less than thirty minutes. As he looked out over St. Paul Place, he saw only a clear blue sky, people going about their business, most, he supposed, talking about the explosion. No one downtown or in its environs, could have escaped hearing, and feeling, the impact of the blast.

He knew that there were fatalities – crew members, longshoremen, and was disappointed with himself for not considering them first. His secretary, when he asked her to hold his calls and visitors, assumed that he was grieving this loss of life. this catastrophe. But his thoughts concerned the effect of the explosion on his business. He was considering finances, the costs to him, his company, how he would pay. He reviewed his investments, considered which to cash in, which to move, studied the specific clauses in the policies regarding terms of payment.

The pain in his abdomen became acute, so sharp that he pushed on his stomach. It's like being stabbed, he thought, a stabbing pain. Such a cliché, he said to himself. Bile surged to the back of his throat. A sciatic pain that had presented itself heretofore only at night shot down his leg with such force that his knee buckled. He caught himself on the window sill.

Good God, he thought. Now even the old body is going. A heart attack, being stabbed, vomiting and sciatica. Maybe it is time to give it up.

At that moment he heard a light tap at the door. Recognizing his secretary's touch, he cleared his throat and stood erect.

"Yes," he called. The door opened quietly. Violet Marsh held a china cup and saucer, the thin white porcelain banded with a thin strip of gold.

"I thought you might like a cup of tea," she said. "Such a shock. Such a shock to the whole city, I should think."

He nodded. She brought the drink to his desk, and left, closing the door soundlessly.

Life goes on, he thought. Another cliché. When you are in a pickle you can always count on clichés. Better than counting on the Bible, or on God, perhaps.

He went to his desk and inhaled the smoky scent of the English tea, then leaned back in the soft brown leather chair, the finest his money could buy. Drawing his pen from its holder, he lifted a sheet of white bond from the second drawer on his left, and buzzed his secretary.

"Bring me the Cottman file."

***

Hollins Street

Helen Aylesforth sat in the front seat of the open car, two blankets wrapped around her legs as she and her son-in-law returned to Hollins Street. "Really, Nicholas, this is not a car for year-round use."

He nodded, but remained silent.

His mother-in-law spoke again. "Well, that was an experience I hope not to repeat. Bodies on stretchers, on the floor, bloody clothing. And the smell, of blood, of death." She sighed. "But no Randolph. And that is a good thing.

"Now for our next steps."

Nicholas turned to face her. "Hospitals. But we must leave that until tomorrow. Meanwhile it is best if you rest, put this experience from your mind."

For Nicholas, there were other issues that he wished he could put from his mind, issues that must be discussed with his father, before the older man learned from someone else, another source.

Helen did not reply. As Nicholas turned the car onto Arlington Street, she faced him. "Please take me to the alley."

***

St. Paul Place

Thirty minutes later, Nicholas rapped lightly on the door to his father's office. Charles Sherwood looked up over his half-glasses, nodded for Nicholas to enter.

"What did you find?" the older man said.

As Nicholas started to answer, he noticed the file on his father's desk. "You're working on the Cottman file? Already?" he asked.

"I want to be in contact with them before they call us, want Cottman to know that we are on it, that they will have no trouble, that we are here to support them." He looked up at his son.

"But tell me about your trip with Mrs. Aylesforth. What did you find?"

"It was more what we didn't find," Nicholas answered. "Arbutus's husband, Randolph, was not among the bodies. That means that he was either hurt and taken to one of the hospitals, or that his body is at the bottom of the harbor. Of course, I told Mrs. Aylesforth it was the former. I did not speak of bodies being swept away, did not want to upset her. But that is a distinct possibility.

"She wanted me to start calling or visiting the hospitals; I told her that I needed to return to the office, that I would be in touch with her this evening. I left her with Arbutus and her family in the house on the alley. Mrs. Aylesforth said that she would have no trouble returning to her home and I think that is accurate."

He stood by his father's desk. "What are your suggestions on how to proceed? I would like to go to Cantata, to see how she is fairing. She was quite upset when Arbutus just ran out of the house like she did."

Nicholas moved to one of the brown leather armchairs facing his father's desk, waited for his father to speak.

"I think it best if we wait until morning to proceed. If Randolph, that is his name, is being treated for a minor injury, they will see that he is returned home. If it is more than that, then they will be busy with him this evening. Yes, let us give them time for that. Tomorrow will be time enough, and we can determine an efficient way to search for him. I do not think it wise that Helen, Mrs. Aylesforth, go gallivanting through the city as she did. No. Perhaps you can take an hour in the morning before you report here. And take Miss Marsh. Yes, you work it out with her, divide the hospitals between the two of you. Do that before you come in. That way we will have it completed and we all can get back to normal. Please inform Mrs. Aylesforth of our decision. She, and Arbutus, should remain at home until they hear from us. It would not do for a woman to be out after dark. If he were taken to Provident, well, his wife can go there in the morning. If he had a major injury, he would have been taken to Hopkins, perhaps Church Home and Infirmary, more likely Mercy Hospital. Somewhere in the downtown area. So we can, or rather, you can, concentrate your efforts there.

"Of course, if he is not found, we must assume that he has perished. Then you can help the woman with her next steps. I was given to understand that he was a stevedore, is that correct? There may be some payments if all was in order. You can help them with that.

"Meanwhile, I have not found the reinsurance certificate on the Cottman account. It should be part of the file. Did you, perhaps, neglect to send it to Johnston when you authorized payment?"

Nicholas had hoped to talk to his father before this item was brought up. He stood, addressed his father. "Let me check in my files, sir. I will let you know within the hour."

As Nicholas walked back to his office, he knew there would be no insurance certificate. Edward Johnston had reminded him several times before year's end that the premium was due, that he needed to authorize payment. Reinsurance on the Cottman Account, less than $100 premium. The invoice had become buried in the piles of papers on his desk. He had known it was there somewhere, but didn't take time to look. Shortly after the first of the year, he had swept the pile into the right-hand bottom drawer. Why did I do that? he asked himself.

He realized that, at this point, it didn't matter. What did matter is that the premium had not been paid, that there was no reinsurance on the Cottman account, and that the firm was responsible for the full amount of the loss. What did matter is that the error was entirely his. What did matter is that he hadn't told his father. What did matter is that he must inform him, that putting it off would only make matters worse.

What did matter was that he knew that he was a coward, and that he could not afford to be one any longer.

March 8, 1913

St. Paul Place

At nine o'clock the next morning, Charles Sherwood's chair was turned to the window facing east. His eyes were closed. He started when the telephone on his desk rang.

"It's Violet on the line, Mr. Sherwood."

"Violet?"

"I mean Miss Marsh. She's asked to speak to you, sir."

The girl has no manners, he thought. Violet, indeed. He would have Miss Marsh speak to her. "Yes, put her through. Put Miss Marsh through immediately."

She began to speak, not waiting for a word from her superior. "I have found him, Mr. Sherwood. Randolph Corporal, that is. He's in Mercy Hospital. It was the first one I visited. He is in the Colored Ward. Some kind of concussion. They said that he knew his name was Randolph, that he couldn't remember his last name or where he lived, but they say that his memory should return. They haven't looked in on him yet this morning."

"Well, that is good news," Sherwood said. "Please report to the office. I will call Mrs. Aylesforth and let her know that he has been found and is safe."

"Don't hang up yet, Mr. Sherwood. There is more." Violet rushed to speak, afraid that her employer would end the call before she had a chance to continue.

"There is more," she repeated, and sensed Sherwood's impatience through the wire. "Sir, the doctor said that he has lost a leg and some

42

fingers, that he should recover from the blow to the head, but there is more to his recuperation. They would like to speak to a family member about how to proceed."

"Well, this is quite another story than the one you first presented." Sherwood paused. "But thank you. And tell the doctor, or whomever you talked to, that we will notify the family, they don't have to worry about that, and that we will determine how best to proceed. Tell them that I or Mrs. Aylesforth will be in touch, most likely Mrs. Aylesforth."

He hesitated. "Tell them that you want to see the boy, the man. Then tell him not to worry, that we will be determining what is the best thing for him, that we will inform his family this morning. See if they will allow you to do that. Then, Miss Marsh, please return as soon as that task is completed. There is much work that awaits you."

Violet replaced the earpiece and followed her employer's instructions.

March 9, 1913

Hollins Street

"We will bring him here for his initial recovery," Helen Aylesforth said. She sat at the dining room table while Myrtle set the tray on the sideboard. "You may tell Arbutus."

"Miss Helen, I don't know if Arbutus will want that. She talks about that he will be in our house. I'm thinking that's what she plans." Myrtle knew that there was a storm brewing, one that she did not want to be part of. She also knew that the day would be long and hard.

"Nonsense. I will talk with Arbutus. She can come here each day, take care of him here. That way your home will not be disrupted, the children can go on with their lives. Randolph will recover in a more restful environment. Surely you see that, do you not?"

"Oh, Miss Helen, please don't get me in the middle between you and 'Butus. You both know what is right, I expect. I will do my best no matter what."

"Yes. I understand you. Arbutus is strong-willed. Most times that is a good thing. It would not be a good thing were she to be strong-willed now, when I obviously know best and have her interests in mind.

"Yes. Please find her and send her to me."

Myrtle sighed. A battle ahead, she thought, that only one person can win. She hoped that Arbutus would see it that way. "I will, Miss Helen. 'Butus is at the hospital now, with Randolph. I'm hoping that someone there will tell her what will happen with him, when he can come home, where he will go." She closed her lips, realizing that her last phrase would have been better left unsaid.

"No question about where he will go, Myrtle. The question is how will he find a life for himself, for his family. I can help with that. You tell Arbutus."

When Myrtle left the house, Helen went to the telephone, contacted her son-in-law.

"Nicholas, I want you to find out just what benefits are due Randolph. I believe that the Longshoreman's Union has something there, for longshoremen, at least. Will you tell me if a stevedore would come under that category? Do you know? Will you find out for me? It is a matter of grave importance, as I'm sure you realize. I would like this information at your earliest convenience. Please call me when you have information. I will be here waiting for your response."

Nicholas told his mother-in-law that he would get back to her, reminding her that it was a Sunday, after all, that it might be Monday or Tuesday before he could learn anything, but that it was high on his list.

Higher, however, was the need to talk to his father, to face his father with his mistake.

March 15, 1913

Hollins Street

The following week, Helen Aylesforth was completing her morning toilette when she heard the phone ring. How inappropriate to phone this early, she thought, and considered allowing the phone to continue to ring. Highly inappropriate, she decided.

The ringing stopped and then started again. Sighing, Helen descended the stairs and picked up the receiver.

Before she could speak, Cantata began. "Mother, Nicholas has just told me that you intend to bring Randolph into our home. Is this true? Do you know how unsuitable that is? What are you thinking? What in the world is wrong with you?"

Helen stepped back from the receiver, lowered the earpiece to her waist, pressed her lips tightly together.

"Mother, are you there? Are you listening to me?"

Helen moved to the small wooden chair by the staircase, waited for her pulse to slow before she responded.

"My dear Cantata, may I remind you to whom you are speaking? Your rudeness is unacceptable. Before we speak further, you will apologize or this call will end. Do you understand me? And I might remind you that the home to which you refer is *my* home."

Cantata brought her fist to her thigh, fought back tears. "Mother, why can't you listen to me. I am saying this for your own good. It is --"

Helen interrupted her. "I am waiting for your apology, Cantata. You will do that if we are to continue this conversation."

"I apologize." Cantata cried into the receiver. "I don't know why you can't listen to me? Why you can't hear what I have to say." Her last words were garbled, caught in her throat.

Helen rubbed her left temple, felt tears in her own eyes. She inhaled deeply before she spoke. "Cantata, what is it? What do you have to say? I did not think that I had to put my decision before you for your approval. I have decided that Randolph will stay here for the first weeks of his recovery. Arbutus will care for him. He will be no trouble for me, and his being here will allow their household, and their children, to operate as close to normal as they can, with a father who has been severely injured and with no immediate means of support.

"You must consider that, Cantata. You have lived a providential life. You know nothing of privation. His being here for a few weeks will not harm anyone, and may provide some good, some solace, to those who might need it. You must think of others and not be so self-centered. That will come to no good, you should know that by now."

Cantata, swallowed hard before she spoke. "I am not thinking of myself in this, Mother, but of you, the damage to your reputation from having a colored man in your house, living in your house with you there alone. And the danger that he might harm you, might steal from you."

Helen looked up the stairs, concentrated on the red pattern that lay deep in the navy carpet. "Cantata, let us leave it as it is. Arbutus will continue to come to Calvert Street two days a week. Let us say nothing more about Randolph."

Cantata's tears started again. "Why is it that there is always someone else who comes first with you? Why can you not put me, my feelings, me, first? You have never done that, not even when Papa was alive. Something, someone always came first."

"Cantata, you are a grown woman. It is time to put those childish ravings aside. You are a mother, and you have a good life. No need to go over the past.

"It is best that we say goodbye. I will be in contact with you. Perhaps you could come here for tea, next week, or the week after."

★★★

The Alley, Hollins Street

"I want him here, Mama, with us, with the children around him. That's how he'll get better, not bein' all quiet in that big house with Miss Helen tellin' him to read books. He's not Wanderer, Mama. That quiet, no, that won't do no good for Randolph."

Myrtle had known that Arbutus would think this way, would not want Randolph to go to the big house, even for a few days.

"'Butus, she's got her mind made up. You know how she is; she's like you. There's no talkin' to her when she's like this."

Camelia brought the teapot over to the table, put it out in front to them. Arbutus pushed it away. "I don't care, Mama. This is one time when I am not giving in. I'm not."

Myrtle stood. "'Butus, we can't afford to offend her, not now. We need her to watch out for us, 'specially now with Randolph like he is. You need to think about Wanderer, Lillian Gish. Who's goin' to look out for them, if not Miss Helen?"

"Mama, stop it. Just stop it. We don't need her. We don't need her if she can just tell us what to do, like we were still her slaves. This is 1913, not 1813."

Myrtle stood, unwilling to hear her employer disparaged. "How can you say that? She been nothin' but good to us, to you, to Wanderer. I knowed her since she was a baby. She is good to us, has always been. Oh, sometimes she be bossy, but that's how it is. That's what we pay for bein' taken care of like we are. And now this is just one more thing. She's doin' it from a good heart. Think of that, 'Butus.

"And it would just be for a few days, a week or so. You can do that, can't you? You'll see, she'll fix things up for us, get us through this. You'll see."

That afternoon, Arbutus arrived at the basement floor of Mercy Hospital, was led to the cot where Randolph lay. She told him of the plan. He turned his face away from her. "I don't care where I go, jus' so I's left alone."

"Randolph, that's not like something I'd hear from you. Why would you talk like that, say such a thing, with me, Wanderer, Mama, all at home waiting for you?"

"Don't no body want no one-legged nigger. Not even all his fingers. Don't no one want that. Jes' leave me here."

April 20, 1913

Hollins Street

Randolph went from the hospital to the second floor, back room, of the big house. From his bed he could see through the yard to the house facing the alley. He thought of it, after all those years, as home. He missed it, although here, ensconced in the high bed, with pillows, linen sheets, fine soft blankets, Arbutus and Myrtle, sometimes even Helen Aylesforth, fussed over him, served him. Like some kind of sultan – that's what Wanderer had said, then told him what a sultan was.

"That boy is way smarter than me," he told Arbutus one morning three weeks into his stay as she delivered his breakfast tray. "And look at this coffee pot. Silver." He smiled, the first Arbutus had seen since the day, the day they referred to as "the accident."

"Here I am, using fine china and drinking from a silver pot. Bet your mama would have never believed this."

Arbutus beamed and sat on the narrow bed. "You feelin' better? I haven't seen you smile since, well, for a long time."

"I'm smiling because I'm goin' home today. Miss Helen's doctor comin' this afternoon, and he's promised that I can get out of jail. Just so's I can use these crutches, which I can."

"Hush. You'll be done for if Miss Helen hear you talk. This is some jail, Randolph, silver coffee pots and meals delivered."

"Too much time to think, all alone up here, 'Butus. She keeps bringin' books. She wants to take me over, like she done Wanderer. But I ain't no Wanderer."

"She's looking after you. That's what she does. She has nothing else to fill her time. Can't you see that?"

Randolph was quiet, the smile gone from his lips, his eyes. "And what will fill my time?" he said, to no one in particular.

Arbutus considered responding, but rose from the bed and went to the window. "Lilacs will be blooming soon," she said, though she knew it would be weeks before that scent would make itself known.

Downstairs, Helen Aylesforth stood in the hallway, telephone receiver in hand, earpiece raised.

"Nicholas, I have some items for you to research. First, I paid Randolph's hospital bill. I would think that Cottman should cover that. You have some kind of connection there, I believe. Please ensure that I am refunded my payment. I believe that you can handle that for me, can you not?"

Without stopping, or giving her son-in-law a chance to respond, she continued. "Also, Randolph may be leaving today, to go back to his home. I think that Cottman should pay something to the family, for his injuries, his disfigurement. Is there not some kind of fund I read about? I think I mentioned that to you before and asked you to find out about it. Yes, please do that. Also, how would we go about collecting, and from whom?" She paused. "Yes, I think that is all for you today."

Nicholas stood by his desk, eyes closed. How much to take on, he wondered, then decided. Not his mother-in-law, not today. "Yes, Mother Aylesforth. I will get back to you."

He replaced the earpiece and returned the phone to the left-hand corner of his desk. Tugging to straighten the cuffs of his jacket, he left his office. As his walked by Miss Marsh's desk, he slowed his pace. "I am gone for the day, should Mr. Sherwood, senior, ask."

He left the building without looking back.

***

Calvert Street

Ten minutes later he turned into the alleyway and pulled the car onto the graveled section of the yard. Paving would have to wait now, he thought. A lot of things would have to wait.

But there was one thing that could not be put off. Nicholas stood before the back door, his father's words of weeks before echoing in his brain.

"A character flaw, Nicholas, a major character flaw. We have discussed this before, more than once. It is bad enough, a disaster, truth be told, that your neglect of this simple task, this miniscule task, has brought us to this, this," Charles Sherwood searched for his words. He hesitated, willed himself to be calm, measured, in his speech. He cleared his throat, busied himself with cleaning his glasses, using the sharply pressed linen handkerchief he always carried. "This disaster," he concluded.

He fixed his eyes on his son. He saw that Nicholas was anxious. As he should be, the senior Sherwood thought. He wanted his son to be aware of his fury. "I can forgive a mistake, an honest one, even a lazy one," Here he paused, intending his son to register the stress he had put on his last words. "But to keep it from me, to hide it, not to admit to it and see to it that it was fixed, before this cataclysm. That may be unforgivable."

He turned away, faced the window. "I don't know why in heaven's name. A check, that is all it took, just a word to Johnston. And then involving him in your duplicity, knowing that you were placing him in an untenable position. What were you thinking, boy?" Charles turned to face his son.

"What were you thinking?

When he received no reply, he said, "I am asking you, Nicholas. That was not a rhetorical question. I am not wasting words this day."

Nicholas sat in the leather chair. The span of his father's desk seemed as wide as the harbor to the south. "It was wrong of me, stupid. I know that." He paused, then looked at his father. "I didn't want to admit that I had failed, that I had let something slide. And yes, you are right, it was from laziness, I guess, at first. And then, yes, cowardice. I can't tell you why I did it, what I was thinking."

Nicholas struggled to keep his voice even. "I know that I have disappointed you. I am sorry. I will do whatever you suggest to make it right."

"Whatever I suggest?" Charles responded. "Whatever I suggest? It is you who should come to me with a solution, not I who continue to tell you what to do. You are a man. Act, think, like one."

Charles reached for his pen, then looked up at his son.

"We have had enough for this morning. Please see me after lunch with your plan."

Nicholas had presented his proposal to his father the following day. But on this Monday afternoon, his task was to inform his wife.

★★★

Park Avenue

Alice Sherwood reached to take her husband's hand. The couple had finished their light dinner – a chop, mashed potatoes, gravy and green beans. Zenobia was their only servant now, and she had prepared their dinner before her late afternoon departure. It was left to Alice to clear the table each night, to place the dishes in the dumbwaiter. Zenobia would take care of them in the morning. She worked six days a week, but didn't mind. The work was not difficult; she had the use of the chauffeur for her errands. Just like a lady, she told her friends.

The Sherwoods dined out on Sunday afternoons. Most often they ventured downtown, to the dining room at the Rennert Hotel, sometimes over to Charles Street, to the Belvedere. For special occasions Charles liked the *Deutches Haus*. He was partial to the food there, though he wished there weren't so many Germans about. The couple ate in the restaurant on the upper floor; they would not venture below to the Rathskeller. In fair weather the aging couple walked. Both enjoyed seeing their city in its lively post-fire resurrection.

But this evening they sat quietly. Charles, laying his cutlery at exactly 180 degrees across his plate, cleared his throat.

"A serious matter to discuss, rather, to tell you about."

Alice watched her husband. Business, she thought. Or his health. That heartburn. She put her right hand to her chest.

"Yes, Charles. What is it? I'm listening. Is it your health? Is that it? Is something wrong?"

She waited, knew not to chatter on, willed herself to be silent, not to allow her nervousness to overtake her.

And so Charles told her of the error, Nicholas's error, using the term "oversight." He spoke of the reputation of the firm, of his commitment to integrity, to doing the right thing.

She was quiet, nodding in silent agreement as he spoke.

"We, or rather I, and you," he added too late for her not to notice, "have sufficient funds, personal funds, to honor the firm's commitment. And that I intend to do.

"It will not be pleasant for us; we will have no cushion, so to speak, but I do believe that, in time, we may live more comfortably than in these next years ahead."

He put his hands over those of his wife's. "I am sorry to have to bring this to you."

"No more violet creams, for a while at least." Alice smiled. "I'm glad I bought those two extra boxes at Christmas." Her throat was dry as she spoke. She hoped that her words weren't heard as a croak.

She saw her husband's eyes fill even as he smiled at her spirited reply. She continued, not giving him a chance to speak. "And are we not fortunate that our needs are few?"

The couple sat without speaking, each with thoughts of the other, of their years together. Unspoken was their knowledge that their years ahead were numbered, most likely too few to recover financially.

Alice looked at her husband. "And what about Nicholas? And his oversight?"

May 7, 1913

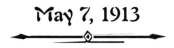

Calvert Street

Arbutus shook her carpet bag as the streetcar came to its stop on Calvert Street. Cantata was due for a fitting, a final one, on the silk and lace tea dress that she had commissioned weeks ago. Arbutus also had with her a dress for the little one; she had finished the baby-blue smocking on the white dotted-swiss pinafore the night before.

Her scissors clanked against the tin filled with straight pins. Arbutus had bought special pins, despite the expense. Extra-long, with round yellow heads, so that fittings would be easier on her fingers. Not so many punctures, though the pricks hurt less these days. Her fingertips were becoming calloused, she realized. Must rub some salve in them every night, she reminded herself, then remembered last night, with Randolph.

She thought that he would see things in a more positive light once he returned home, once they shared a bed again, once the bandages were removed. He'd be with family, with Wanderer talking to him, telling him of the adventures he was reading about, maybe even get Randolph interested in reading. Miss Helen would like that.

He could spend time with Lillian Gish, she hoped, help the child to come out of herself, wean her away from Camelia. Arbutus shook her head and thought. The child sticks to Camelia like a mustard plaster. Yes, that child needs to get hold of herself, find herself some personality if she's to survive in this world, this world that throws its worst at you just when you think things will work out.

She had been certain that Randolph would be better once they were together at night, just the two of them, like before. But since he had returned home, he had not reached for her, and she, shy, unsure, had said nothing. Last night, she had made sure that she was ready, had moved gently toward him, pressed herself against his back, laid her hand on the nape of his neck, moved her head near his. But he had shifted his body so that her hand no longer touched him. "No more," he said. "Not until I'm a man." And he had not responded to her whispers.

Well, that's what you get, she thought, being careful as she stepped off the curb, remembering her trip to Kresge's the day before the accident. The accident, the day before her world turned upside down. Mama was right. Be careful of the good. The bad don't like it and it always wins in the end. Special pins, they let me shop there because I work for white people. And now this.

She climbed the four marble steps, rapped the brass door knocker attached to the heavy black door. She knew that Cantata was aware that she used the front entrance now, that she was no longer a servant consigned to using the alleyway to get to the back door. I am a *modiste*, she thought, grateful that Miss Helen had taught her that word. French, it was. Yes, Miss Helen would be proud of me, she thought, as Meg opened the door to let her in.

She greeted Meg, and went directly to the front room to wait for Cantata. Still lost in her thoughts, she stopped, squared her shoulders, made sure that she was standing tall. You confront what you have, then make a plan, she decided. That's what Miss Helen had said to her, that chat in her front room, Randolph still in the bed upstairs in the big house, the morning before he had come back to the house, back home, weeks now.

Pressing her lips together, she waited, hoping that Cantata would be late as usual. That would give her a few minutes to herself. Her thoughts returned to that Wednesday when she was summoned to the front room. She heard Mrs. Aylesforth's voice, remembered that tone of voice. Arbutus knew it was something important.

"Arbutus," Helen Aylesforth had said as she heard Arbutus come down the stairway. "Let us sit and discuss some things." The older woman opened the pocket doors to the front room.

Two Boston ferns spilled over the lace-covered mahogany table in the bay window that fronted Hollins Street. A silver tea service sat on the table in front of the upholstered horsehair sofa.

Helen signaled to Arbutus to sit, a wave of the hand that she did not consider imperious, although her audience always did. "I had your mother lay out the service while you were with Randolph."

Arbutus sat, unsure of where the conversation would lead. Miss Helen had not wanted any dresses made for months. And something was afoot with Miss Cantata, something going on in that house. Arbutus felt that Meg had a hint, a clue, an intimation of what it was, but she and Arbutus never talked. On the days that Arbutus sewed for the family, Meg laid her lunch out on the kitchen table, but was never present when Arbutus ate. A good meal it was, Arbutus remembered, the table set with china and silver, though she did notice that the plates were chipped or cracked and the tines of the forks at times bent.

Arbutus nodded to Mrs. Aylesforth, sat on the edge of the sofa. She wouldn't be telling me that I was no longer needed. She wouldn't do that, not now, with Randolph right in her house.

And indeed, Helen Aylesforth did not do that. Rather she presented Arbutus with an intriguing proposal.

As she handed the thin china cup, Shelley Rosebud pattern, to Arbutus, Helen Aylesforth said, "Do you remember doing this when you were a little girl? Just like this, Arbutus. It's been many years since we've done this, has it not?"

Arbutus nodded, smiled, thought back to the years when Mrs. Aylesforth had her classes. Etiquette lessons, she called them.

Her teacup poised on her knees, Arbutus remembered those times, recalled Miss Helen's voice.

"Arbutus, you have a gift, something special. You can go far if you so choose, and I want you to know how to behave. That way, the regard that is your due will come to you. People will grant you respect without even knowing that they are doing it. It is inherent in how you carry yourself, in how you conduct yourself."

Solomon and James had made fun of her. "Gettin' above your station. You better watch out for that, girl," they'd tell her, Solomon prancing about with a book on his head. She'd run to them and push them, hard. That just made them laugh more. And where are they today, she wondered, and wished them safe, though they surely would have contacted Mama if they were. Still, she wished them safe; she wished them alive.

Helen cleared her throat, and Arbutus was brought back to the present. She looked down at her tea, brought the cup to her lips, the liquid now cool enough now to drink small sips, as Mrs. Aylesforth had instructed, all those years ago.

"Now, I am sure you are wondering why I want to see you.

"First of all, it is not about Randolph. He is welcome to stay here as long as is necessary, although I do believe that he is anxious to be in his own home. That is understandable. But, it is you and your future that I would like to discuss this afternoon."

Helen Aylesforth placed the cup and saucer on the table to her right.

Arbutus waited, nervously knotting the lace handkerchief, a birthday gift from Mrs. Aylesforth some years before, that she had taken from the pocket of her navy serge skirt. Sure that she was being dismissed, and fighting the strong urge to lower her gaze, she forced herself to meet her employer's eyes.

Helen Aylesforth noticed this and silently congratulated herself on instilling a doughty strength in the woman who sat before her.

"Arbutus, I will come directly to the point. You are capable of much more than you are doing, making a few dresses for me each year, which, I might add, I do not need. Sewing for Cantata and her friends. Well, that is a start, but you are capable of more. And being around those silly women is not helping your brain.

"Now, you are also in a bit of a pickle due to Randolph's accident. I will be frank. His earning potential is even more limited than it was before the accident. I am working with my son-in-law to see if there is any possibility of a payment from Randolph's employer, but it appears that it may be an almost impossible task. And if I, or rather we, are to continue to pursue it, we would have to engage someone else. Mr. Sherwood, junior, informs me that his father's firm is a business partner of sorts with Randolph's employer. So you can see how that would not do."

Arbutus willed herself to listen, though the sounds of her own heart pounding rang in her ears.

Helen took a breath, looked into Arbutus's eyes. "So, you see, now it will be up to you. To be the breadwinner, so to speak."

Arbutus felt her mouth go dry. Was Mrs. Aylesforth telling her that she had to take her mother's place, to be a servant in the big house? All that reading? All that arithmetic, to be a servant, just like her mother? Arbutus felt her eyes fill.

Helen Aylesforth noticed this as well.

"No need to be soft, Arbutus. You cannot afford to be soft. No, you must face life. It is what separates the strong from the weak."

Arbutus swallowed, picked up her tea cup, looked down into it, this time not meeting Mrs. Aylesforth's gaze.

"Now, here is the plan." Mrs. Aylesforth showed a rare smile. "You will have a business, a dress-making business, with a proper shop and showroom.

"What do you think of that!"

Sitting in the Sherwood's front room, Arbutus smiled at the memory. A proper shop she would have. Miss Helen would help her. A proper shop, with fabric and lace and pins, all with round heads. And perhaps a helper.

She heard Cantata coming down the hall staircase. Cantata was humming.

Strange, Arbutus thought.

June 3, 1913

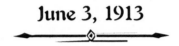

The Alley, Hollins Street

"Pops, tell me about Deadwood Dick. Tell me that story again."

Randolf pulled Wanderer onto the bed. "You love that story, don't you? You think you can be Deadwood Dick? You want to follow his footsteps, get yourself shot?"

"He survived, Pops, don't forget. He got the best of all of them. He was a hero. That's what I'm goin' to be. A hero. A real hero. Out West. Not stayin' in the East, no. I'm gonna be a cowboy, out West, Like Deadwood."

"You a Wanderer, all right. Miss Myrtle had a good name for you. Wanderer."

"So, tell me, Pops. You tell it to me again. I want to write it down this time. Take it to school with me, read it to the class. Miss Barnslow said I could. She did, Pops. She said I'm the smartest one in the class. She said that, and not just to me."

Randolph pushed himself up, sat taller. "She, that Miss Barnslow, is a fine judge of character, boy. A fine judge." He smiled, the widest smile he had shown since before. Wanderer noticed. And he smiled even wider than his father.

"So, here is the story: Nate Love was born a slave, but he learned how to read and write. After he was freed, he found a Texas outfit that had delivered its herd and was preparing to go back. They had some colored cowboys who were already in the outfit. So he asked if he could join. The boss told him that if he could break the wildest horse in the outfit, he could go with them. He chose the wildest horse he could find, the boss man did.

"And what do you think happened?" Randolph watched his son's face. They both knew this story.

Wanderer called out, "He got that horse tamed. He got that horse to let him ride, just like that!"

"Right you are. And then, somehow, Nate got hold of a gun, and practiced and practiced. And eventually he could shoot better than anybody there."

Randolph shifted his weight to the right, straightened out his remaining leg. Wanderer smoothed the sheet, just like he had seen his mother and grandmother do. He watched his father, saw him grimace.

Randolph cleared his throat, coughed, then continued. "Then he got a job in Arizona where he learned to speak Mexican, from working with the cowboys there."

"The Mexican cowboys are called *vaqueros*, Pops," Wanderer said, not able to keep this bit of information to himself, though he knew his interrupting would irritate his father.

"Now, do you want me to tell this story or not, boy? Save all your fancy learning for school. I'm tellin' this story now."

Wanderer smiled, as did Randolph. "Okay, Pops. You're the storyteller today."

"So, to continue," Randolph said. "Nate's outfit received orders to deliver three thousand steer to Deadwood City, and when they arrived he found out about a contest with $200 prize money. The one who could tame a mustang horse in the shortest time would win.

"Well, Nate got that horse so that he could ride it in nine minutes flat. That is the truth. Nine minutes exactly. Then next he had to shoot, and he made all bullseyes one hundred percent of the time. All bullseyes. The town had never seen anything like it, so's they gave him the name Deadwood Dick. And the prize money, of course."

"Tell me the rest. That isn't the end. You know that!"

Randolph put his hand out, rubbed the top of his son's head. "So, no, that is not the end. So here is old Deadwood, and what do you think happens to him?"

"Indians," Wanderer shouted.

"Yes, Indians. He gets shot fourteen times, but he gets away. Then, later, he tries to steal a US Army cannon. Don't know what he thought he'd do with a cannon. Crazy, I guess he was." Randolph leaned back and laughed.

"Then there was the time he rode into a bar in Mexico and ordered two drinks – one for him, the other for his horse."

"And they gave it to him," Wanderer shouted. "That is my favorite part. They gave his horse a drink. A colored man like Deadwood Dick, they had to do what he told them to do.

"That's goin' to be me. People are goin' to do what I tell 'em."

"Boy, you watch how you go about that dream, so's you don't end up on the wrong end of a noose."

"Oh, I'm not stayin' around here, Pops. No sir. I'm heading out."

Randolf looked over at his son. "You are a wanderer, my boy. That is for sure."

"You bet, Pops. Wanderer. That's who I am, and that's what I'm going to do."

PART II
New Year's Eve, 1913

---◇---

The Alley, Hollins Street

Wanderer sat by the kitchen stove. Myrtle looked over the black-eye peas and greens, simmering on the stove. "You make them only on New Year's, Gramam?" he asked.

"Oh Laws, I guess you're right. Forgot about them until yesterday, and had to run to the market to grab the last bunches of greens. They should really cook a couple of days, so's they can stew in that pot likker. But this year, well, you know, Wanderer, this has been another kind of year for us. I should have made black-eye peas and greens a lot more. It might have warded off our trouble. That trouble has come to our doorstep to be sure. More prayin' needed. That's how we need to bring in the year. Ain't I right, Melie?"

An hour later, Myrtle stood firm, both hands placed on the table. "No. No blood money is comin' into this house. That is my final word. Blood money will only bring more misery. That I know. Knowed it since Joshua. He tol' that to me, I remember it. I keep his word.

"Blood money, don't you see that 'Butus? Not in my house. No." Myrtle's voice shook on her last words. Nothing but trouble this year, she thought. Now here is 'Butus wanting to bring in more. We can manage; we always have. We don't need money that bad. What good would it do anyway? No, 'Butus, Randolph, they need to think of the future, not just reach out to something handed to them for no good. I will take a stand, no matter what Miss Helen says, no matter how angry 'Butus gets.

"This isn't your house, Mama. We live here because of Miss Helen. You need to listen to what she says. This the first time you haven't. I don't know what's wrong with you. That money's due Randolph, due to him, Mama. Can't you see that? There's no blood money here. There's no such thing as blood money. Miss Helen helped to get us this. Why would you stand against her? She won't like that, you know. Won't like it a bit."

Arbutus knew that her only chance to get her mother to change her mind was to remind her of what Helen Aylesforth wanted for them. She was mystified that Myrtle would go against her employer. But, here Mama is, Arbutus thought, sticking to her guns, as Wanderer would say.

She turned and put on her coat. She would go to the big house, see Miss Helen. Yes, Miss Helen will lay down the law, she thought, make Mama come to her senses.

Helen was standing by the window in the back room when she noticed Arbutus coming to the house, knew by her pace that that something was amiss. She had the back door opened by the time Arbutus got to the steps. "Come in, Arbutus. You look like you have something on your mind. We can have tea while you tell me what is wrong." The two went downstairs to the kitchen; Arbutus fixed the tea, warmed the cups before she sat.

Helen listened, paused before she responded. "There is no use adding to dissension in your house, Arbutus. All of you there, living so close. There is enough sadness, enough trouble. Let us not add to it. The atmosphere must be one where Wanderer can continue his reading, his studies. That is the most important factor."

The older woman sat, stared ahead. Arbutus knew that she was devising a solution.

"We can use that money, Arbutus. Put it to good use, without actually having it go to you, to Randolph, directly." She turned to face her guest. "We can use it to start your business. Yes, the time is right, I think. After the first of the year, we will find you a place. We must think of a name. And we will advertise. Meanwhile, you start building up your samples. In business it is called inventory, I think. But yes, samples. Some of your designs that customers can see when they come to the shop. They'd be able to choose fabrics, colors that they wanted, but would have the samples right there for them to see. They wouldn't have to rely on drawings, patterns." She drew in a breath, placed her palms flat on the table as she rose.

"So, that is decided. You have your work cut out for you these next months. You can use the upstairs room whenever you'd like, come and go as you please. Purchase whatever fabrics and such as you think best. I'll handle the bills for now. But the business will be yours.

"Arbutus, 1914 will be your year. I will see to that!"

★★★

Park Avenue

"Violet creams on New Year's Eve. Not a bad way to end the year, I think." Alice Sherwood carried the cut-glass dish into the front room.

Charles sat in the crimson damask chair, smoothed the crocheted antimacassars on both its arms. He noticed that frost was beginning to form at the corners of the front windows. "Cold night out there, a very good night to be at home. To bring in the new year snug. With the woman I'd most like to be with." He smiled as he took a chocolate from the plate.

"Is this the end of your treasured candies? Or are there more special occasions where you'll bring out one or two?"

Alice knew what her husband was thinking. "It hasn't been so bad, has it? Aren't we fortunate to be at a time in our lives where what is important is measured in time, not things. Except for violet creams."

Charles reached for her, drew her closer. "It has been a year that I would not like to repeat. Perhaps the worst of my life, or perhaps the memories of other horrible years fade with time, with age."

Charles thought back to the afternoon, closing the office early, giving the staff a few extra hours. Johnston, always quiet, even more so since the explosion, had come in to apologize once again; he cast blame on no one except himself. A gentleman, thought the elder Sherwood, a man of character. Someone he wanted to keep close, an asset to the firm. Miss Marsh, quiet as always, doing her job, never letting on that she knew the situation between her employer and his son. And that new switchboard operator, better than the other one. Charles could not remember her name. Just as well she had resigned, married, he thought, or something like that. No, this one was much better, more circumspect. That other one, no breeding, didn't know her place, and at the switchboard too. She could know more than he was comfortable with, able to listen in on calls.

No, she would not have done at all. Good for her to be gone. He thought that he would find out the other one's name, the new one, make a point of speaking to her sometime.

New Year's resolutions, he thought, makes you feel young again, that there is always the future, always time to change, always time to do better.

He was sure that those who knew of the firm's, of his, financial difficulties were few. The payment to Cottman had been made within days of the claim. Clients noted that; the reputation of the firm remained solid. He had kept George on the payroll, to let the chauffeur go would have been an all too public indication of problems, but he had cut back his hours, and given him employment prospects to pursue. If he did leave, Charles had decided not to replace him, not for the near future at least. Perhaps he would even sell the car. He would consider how that might look to business associates.

Christmas gifts made to customers, fruit baskets from Hopper McGaw, towering tins of confections from Lexington Market; the police on the beat, the firemen at the nearby stations, all received their fifth of Pikesville Rye. It was not a bad Christmas, Charles thought, even with …

He interrupted his thoughts to look over at his wife. Alice sat on the sofa, staring into the fire. Zenobia had laid it before she had left for the day. Alice had lit it after dinner.

"What say we take a trip in 1914? Germany maybe? In the spring."

Alice looked at the wall over the mantle, the slight outline of the painting that had hung there faintly visible, to those who knew. She leaned forward to pour sherry into the small glass on the silver tray. "Are you thinking of the Telser? Do you miss it?"

Sherwood turned in his chair, put his hands on his knees. "I suppose so. Or perhaps it is that every time I see that empty space, it brings it all back to me. Selling that painting, bought during such a happy time for us. It always reminded me of you, with Nicholas, with Susannah, all that gold hair. Brought such romantic thoughts. Silly, now that I think of it.

"No, I don't miss the painting; I'm just saddened that I've brought all of this on you, at a time that was to be one without worry for us."

Alice rose, put her hand on her husband's head. "This is a fine time for me, for us. We have our health. We have enough, Charles. How blessed we are to have enough."

He looked over at his wife. You are my blessing, he thought. He stood. "Let's go to the back door, look out at this last night of 1913."

The couple walked to the back of the house, stood at the open door, watched the stars in the darkened sky to the west. "Yes," Charles said. "I think we could manage a trip to Germany, second class if you don't mind. Perhaps a last trip for us. This summer, July, August. To Dresden. I like Germany; too bad it has all those Germans.

"And then a side trip to London, to see Susannah."

★★★

Calvert Street

Cantata stood before the mahogany wardrobe in her bedroom. Another New Year's Eve, she thought. So different from last year, so much change. She put her hand on the yellow velvet hangers. Well, they stay, at least. They'll be here for a long time. And the dresses. They stay. I can wear them. Nicholas was right. I don't need so many, not really.

And tonight, we will have our own celebration. It will be fine; we will be fine. Nicholas did the right thing. That's important. His father recognizes that. He won't keep Nicholas to his agreement. No bonuses? For how long? He can't hold him to that. He'll see that it would hurt his grandchildren. He wouldn't stand for that. She ran her left hand over the green silk tea dress that was closest to her, closing her eyes as she felt the soft coolness of the fabric.

And so for this year coming, it will be a difficult one for us. Then we'll get back to where we were. Anyone can live sparingly for a year. Mr. Sherwood wouldn't make us do without for more than a year. He'll see that Nicholas has learned his lesson. And I have all these dresses, that will make it easier. I'll just say that I'm tired of fashion, so vacuous. Yes, I'll use that word, vacuous.

She pulled out the gown that she had worn last New Year's Eve, relieved that hobble skirts were still in fashion. This will be just fine, she thought. It will be our celebration, just Nicholas and me, like it was in the early days, before the children. Meg agreed to stay on. She can do the cleaning, and the cooking, see to the children. It won't be so bad. We'll get by.

As she turned from the wardrobe, she thought of her mother, that May visit, surprised that she could bring it to mind without crying, or stopping herself from crying. She felt removed from it, as if it was something that she had read about, something that happened in a book, a novel. And, she thought, this last day of the year, this reckoning, this evening, may not be such a bad time to remember it, to consider how that meeting changed me, had made me somehow more adult.

Cantata turned and walked to the bed, sat, stiff-spined. Like Mother, she thought. I have some of her strength. That has come to me. For that, perhaps one day she'll be a bit proud of me.

She closed her eyes, replayed the trip to Hollins Street, saw herself paying the cab driver before she turned to the steps. She had known that Myrtle would not be there, that her mother would be alone. She wanted to be sure that Helen was alone for this meeting.

Nicholas had advised that she visit her mother by herself, without him, said that the two women could talk easier, about the situation, as he termed it. She would tell Helen of Nicholas's solution, that he had promised to repay the full amount of the loss to the firm, over ten years, as long as he could continue to draw his salary, without the bonuses that came every quarter. Those would be paid directly to the company, or to his father, for they both knew that Charles Sherwood had made the payment to Cottman from his own funds.

Cantata had been surprised that her father-in-law had agreed to Nicholas's offer, that he had even drawn up a contract stipulating to the terms of repayment. After all, she thought, when the elder Sherwoods die, Nicholas will certainly inherit the business and at least some of their holdings. His sister Susannah and her husband lived in England, and visited Baltimore only rarely. Their lives were in Europe; surely they would not be interested in the business. And the elder Sherwood would recognize that Nicholas had learned from his mistake, had shown strength of character.

She decided that she would be an understanding wife. She had read stories about wives supporting their husbands in *Woman's Home Companion* and *Ladies' Home Journal*. From what she read, those wives who did not complain, who stood behind their husbands, always came out fine. And that, she determined, would be what she and Nicholas would do. They would come out fine.

No thanks to Mother, Cantata thought, recalling her visit. First, with that Negro staying in the house, being waited on like he was a member of the family. There was no reasoning with her. But once they got over that, with Helen telling her that it was *her* prerogative whom she allowed in her home, once she apologized, as Helen demanded, Cantata was sure that her request, her reasonable request, would be granted. After all, they both knew that when Helen died, the house, the money, everything would be hers. It would come to her eventually, so why would her own mother not want to help them now, when they needed it.

Cantata had given much thought to this visit, what she would say, how she would say it, how long she would wait for her mother to suggest before she would ask, hoping that Helen would offer to make things right, for her grandchildren at least, if not for her and Nicholas. She would not want them to suffer, no grandmother would.

But Helen had sensed that there was something "afoot," as she termed it. She listened as Cantata related the story, Nicholas's offer being accepted, and the financial straits that resulted. Cantata waited, but no offer came. Helen seemed to respect Nicholas's admission of his role in the loss, as well as his plan to repay the company's loss. Cantata knew that her mother would admire that, and had expected that it would put Helen in a generous frame of mind.

Yet her mother remained silent. Cantata felt forced to broach the subject of boarding school for Christopher, saying that she thought it would be better if he were away from the city, where he would not be subject to seeing their deprivations, selling the car, giving up the servants.

"It is not the way that any of his friends live, Mother, you can see that. I don't want him to be ashamed of his family."

Helen merely raised an eyebrow, and wondered how the woman sitting in front of her could have come from her body, have lived in the same house as she, experienced how she and James lived, their values, and yet come away with none of it.

"It might be a good thing for Christopher to experience a bit of real life, to know that all is not a land of milk and honey, to see his parents live up to a standard of character. That could be a very good lesson for him.

"And as for his friends, if they desert him because of his reduced circumstances, they are well behind him. And you, I might add." Helen looked around, as if she were expecting tea to be served, then remembered that Myrtle had left for the day. She turned back to Cantata, tucked a stray wisp of hair back into the knot at the nape of her neck.

"But I will give it some thought. If a boarding school would give him a better education than St. Paul's, that may be worth considering. However, if it is your plan to shelter him from the realities of life, then it would be no favor, to him or to you." She watched her daughter's face, hoping for a sign of connection, of understanding, however slight.

Cantata felt her face flush. "Mother, you have always thought that I have no character, no sense of duty, no understanding of life. I may not read like you do. I may like clothes and things more than you do, but you do me a disservice. You always have. You have no confidence in me, no faith in me. You don't even like me." Cantata's voice was firm, controlled. Even she was surprised that her voice did not shake. She sat, her hands gripping the arms of her chair, and the thought came to her that she would leave perspiration stains there.

"But you underestimate me, Mother. I have not had an easy life, although you would never notice that, or believe it. You have never loved me. And when Jimmy died, you turned on me. After he died, every time you looked at me it was with hatred. You think I didn't see it, but it was impossible not to feel it. You think the wrong one died. Don't you think I know that? How do you think it makes me feel? And if a bit of silk and lace makes me forget that for a while, who are you to sneer at me?

"You spend your time taking care of your Negroes, making sure that they 'live up to their talents,' acting like you are God. Well, you're not. You mean nothing to them. Do you think they like you? All you are is their employer, the one who can give them what they want. You are nothing to them. Nothing. And you are nothing to me." Cantata felt her face burning.

"You can't hurt me anymore. I don't want your money. There isn't enough money in the world to make up for what you've done to me, how you've made me feel. I don't need you. I don't need your money. And my family doesn't need you either." Cantata felt her bowels rumble, stifled her impulse to scream, to strike her mother. She could not stop the flow of words.

She stood, a bit shakily at first, then felt a strength come to her, unbidden. "You have given me a gift, actually. You've taught me how to be a mother. I'll do the exact opposite of everything you've done to me. You stay with Myrtle, and Arbutus, and those children whom you think are so wonderful. Let them be your family, your children. And see how that feels when you lie dying upstairs. Just see how that feels."

And then the sobs came; her nose ran. Cantata put her hand to her face, walked to the corner table and removed her handkerchief from her pocketbook. She turned to see her mother's face.

Helen stood still; she had not moved during the whole of Cantata's confrontation.

"Leave my house. Do not return until you are invited." She turned and mounted the stairs to her bedroom, then stopped. "And I do believe that it would be '*who* you think are so wonderful.' Check your grammar."

Cantata heard the soft click as the door closed. She left the house and chose to walk the twenty-eight blocks home. It took weeks for the blisters on her feet to heal.

★★★

The Alley, Hollins Street

Wanderer slowly placed the bookmark between the pages and laid it on the table. He turned to his mother, who sat in the corner, leafing through the September 1913 issue of *Vogue*.

"Nobody laughs anymore, Mama. I haven't heard any of us laugh in, well, seems like forever."

Arbutus laid the magazine aside, looked over at her son. He was right, she thought. Nobody had laughed, not in those months since the accident. There was nothing to laugh about, Myrtle and Melie with their constant praying, Randolph mostly silent. She too was quiet most of the time, her thoughts focused on planning the outfits to sew, this secret venture, shared only between her and her benefactor, as she thought of Helen Aylesforth, though it was really Randolph's money that would be used, at least in the beginning, until it became a real business.

Time enough later to talk about it. 1914 would be her year, that's what Miss Helen said, and Arbutus believed her. She realized that she had been so taken up with thoughts of being a *modiste* that she hadn't given much thought to Wanderer. She didn't think at all about her daughter, sure that the child was fine, always pushed up beside Melie. But Wanderer, she needed to pay attention to him. He was one to watch. He would go far. She would make sure that happened.

And now he had noticed that no one laughed. She walked to him, stood behind him, placed her hands on his shoulders.

"Oh, Wanderer, you are right. And that is not a good thing for you. Not at all. So we will see what we can do about it." She paused, looked around the house, noticed Randolph's banjo case buried beneath the coats that hung on the peg beside the door.

"Music, Wanderer. That's what we need in this house. Expecially tonight. New Year's Eve. Yes, expecially tonight. I mean *especially* tonight.

"Where's your harmonica, the one that Pops brought you? Get that and we'll figure out a way to get him to play along with you. You and him playin', that's what we all need. Go find it."

Wanderer pushed his book aside. "You know that Gramam tried to find it, to get rid of it. She says that's what caused all this trouble. Pops blasphemin'. You think she'll want music tonight? You think she'll take it from me?"

Arbutus leaned down to kiss the top of her son's head. "Gramam is just tryin' to make sense of things, trying to put a reason for why things happen like they do. So she picked that one thing, when your father made fun of the preacher. But that didn't cause our trouble. Sometimes trouble just comes, nobody done nothin' to cause it, and nothin' nobody can do to make it go away. If it goes, it goes on its own way, when it wants.

"And Pops, he just facin' the days the best way he can. All of us doin' that." She paused, thought about how she had acted, had responded these past months. She hadn't been the best wife to Randolph, so caught up was she in her own plans. Well, a new year, she said to herself. I'd forgotten him. Time to remember.

She rubbed the back of her neck, pulled on the locket that Miss Helen had given her for her sixteenth birthday, sterling silver, it was. "I'll talk to Mama. You go get that harmonica. Tonight, we'll have music. And some smiles."

An hour later, Randolph came in the house. He walked every day; the doctor told him that he had to do that, no sitting stewing. "Out and about, no matter what the weather is. You need to keep your arm strength, build those muscles so that you won't be sore all the time, get used to handling those crutches in all sorts of situations."

Randolph saw the doctor less frequently now. At first it was every month, then every six weeks. Now, after almost nine months, both knew that no more could be done. The incision had not healed completely. It sometimes was red, and it was always weeping. The doctor knew that there was an infection in there, deep, but all he could advise was for Randolph to keep it clean, covered, and apply ointment to keep it from crusting over. As far as the pain, he told Randolph that it would always be there, some days worse than others, and that the best that Randolph could do was to learn to live with it. Laudanum would help. He told Randolph to take it when he felt that he needed it. And whiskey, but he said to watch the whiskey. Cocaine would be a better choice, he said.

Then you live like this, Randolph thought. Watch the whiskey, indeed.

Myrtle had bought some Dr. Gordshell's salve. "Miss Helen used it on a dog she had. Had a sore that just wouldn't heal. Then she tried this, and that sore just disappeared."

Randolph hurt too much to complain. And the salve did help. Me and the goddamned dog, he thought. But it helped. On the worst days, it helped.

His days were spent looking out on the alley, watching those Irish neighbors as they headed to work on the rails. They never acknowledged him or his family when they passed each other in the alley. Nor did he acknowledge them. We were here first, he thought, every time that he saw them. Myrtle, her family, had lived here for years, and now these Irish coming in, building these houses right next to us, taking up all the open fields, taking over.

But this night, as he walked through the door, he was remembering one year ago, and when he looked up, Arbutus stood there, wearing that same green dress. She was holding his banjo. She laid it down and went to him, put her hands on his shoulders.

"We need to celebrate, Randolph. You here alive with us. We all together. That is something to celebrate. I want you to play, like before. I want you and Wanderer to play for us tonight. Music. We need music.

"Wanderer said that none of us laugh anymore. He's right, and we need to change that. This year comin', 1914, this will be a good year for us. I know it."

Wanderer came in from the back room. He had his harmonica and was sounding out notes. Randolph laid down his crutches and hoped to the table. "Come on over here. We'll work on something to play tonight. You and me. A few songs to bring in the new year."

They saw Myrtle walking in from the big house. She heard the music while she was still in the yard. Arbutus stood in the doorway, ready to greet her mother, to be sure that there would be music that night.

She needn't have worried. When Myrtle heard the notes, she smiled. Music, she thought, just what we need.

That night music filled the house on the alley. Helen Aylesforth went to the back room of her second floor. She heard it, and she smiled.

Hours later, Randolph watched as his son settled in for the night. "You did a good thing tonight. You got a gift, Wanderer, a good ear. But now, you need to work on your rhythm. Sink-o-pa-shun. That's what you work on. Listen to this, then you hear it in your sleep, all night. By the time you wake up tomorrow, you'll have it.

"Listen to this -- *be, ba bum, be ba bum, be bum*. You got that? Let's do it together."

And Randolph and his son practiced the uneven rhythm of ragtime, quietly, for by this time Myrtle, Melie and Lillian Gish were asleep in the big bed. When Randolph left his room, Wanderer smiled so wide his teeth dried out. He fell asleep to the sounds of *be, ba bum*, and laughter in his house again.

When Randolph returned to the front room, Arbutus was waiting for him, wearing a lace negligee. It had been Cantata's, but she wasn't thinking of that now.

New Year's Day, 1914

The Alley, Hollins Street

Wanderer woke up early, went outside with his harmonica. He knew he had to play softy as he put the cold metal of the harmonica to his lips. *Be, ba bum, be bum.* Over and over he played, the same note, to that same rhythm, until he didn't have to think so hard about it.

In her bed, Lillian Gish's eyes flew open. She climbed out, careful not to wake Melie, dressed quickly and put on her heavy coat. Once outside, she sat on an upturned bucket and watched. Soon she stood; she couldn't keep her feet from moving. She bobbed with the rhythm, felt her feet, her arms, her body, dance. Wanderer saw her and beckoned her to him. The two, Wanderer playing a song he made up as he went along, danced on this first day of a new year.

Lillian Gish was smiling. Wanderer saw it. He smiled too, so wide that he lost the notes he wanted. Arbutus had come to the back, then had run in to call her mother and Randolph. "Come quick. Look at Lillian Gish. But be quiet, don't let her know you're there."

And they saw the child who never smiled, smile a smile so wide that she felt her mouth stretch as far as it could. It feels good, Lillian Gish thought, and smiled some more.

Then she saw them watching. She put her hand over her mouth, the smile gone. Wanderer kept on playing.

★★★

Hollins Street

Helen Aylesforth stood at the window. Randolph would soon arrive. Must keep up traditions, she thought. Keeping up, yes, keeping up. That is how one got through life. And Myrtle's family would get through this. As would Cantata's.

Interesting, she thought, how life links us. The explosion in the harbor, forgotten now, except by a few. Randolph, Nicholas, one incident, discrete outcomes. And I am the connection. So I must make it right, at least for Myrtle.

She rubbed her hand over the window sill, looked out on Hollins Street. Too early for anyone to be out and about this holiday morning. In a few hours, the street would be busy, cars coming and going, bringing relatives and friends to the neighborhood for their New Year's Open Houses. Not so for her.

Cantata's Christmas card had arrived a few weeks ago. It contained a single printed sentence, wishing the recipient the joys of the holiday season and signed "Cantata and Nicholas." No message.

Helen had not responded. Not yet, she thought. She touched the cold pane of glass. Perhaps in the new year. Perhaps in the new year I'll consider allowing Cantata to begin repairing the damage caused by her outburst. But it will take more than a card, a printed one at that.

Money, always about money. And that nonsense about Jimmy. How could she have spoken that way? To her mother?

Helen considered how one responded in time of trouble to be an indication of character. When trouble had visited Cantata, she took it out on her mother. Well, better that than Nicholas, Helen supposed, although it was Nicholas who brought this on his family. Spoiled, things handed to him too easily, an entitled air about him. Both of them, she thought. Entitled.

She closed her eyes, bit her lips. You spoiled her, James. You did her no favors, always taking her side, coming between us, making my words not count. So of course she went to you, thought that I was the one who didn't care about her. You took up all that space in her heart; there was none left for me. Helen stiffened, then pressed her forehead against the cold glass.

But Jimmy, oh Jimmy, you were the one, the one we knew would be a success, the one everyone loved, who could make everyone laugh. He was the one, James. Helen put her hands to her eyes, forced back her tears. Cantata was right. The wrong one had died.

She blanched when she heard those words in her mind. Still, she told herself, thoughts do not need to be, cannot, in fact, be censured. One has thoughts, yes. That is normal. What matters are one's actions. What matters is how one behaves.

And Helen was sure that her behavior belied her delight in her son, and her disapproval, her irritation, with her daughter. She left the window, walked to the back room. Cantata had no justification in talking to me as she did. None whatsoever. And it will take a lot for her to make it up to me. A lot more than a printed card.

Her thoughts were interrupted when she noticed Randolph coming though the yard. She considered beckoning him to the back door, then decided against it. No, she thought, we must keep things as they were, not give in. And so she watched as he wended his way to the front door. He's become quite adept with those crutches, she thought. Good for him. Yes, grit. Both he and Arbutus have it, although it's closer to the surface with her. Bodes well for Wanderer, good strong stock. He'll go far. And as she thought that, her eyes filled. Oh, Jimmy. I will never forget you, never, never, never.

Helen shook her head, straightened her shoulders, walked to the front door. She had it opened as Randolph arrived at the bottom step.

"Oh, yes, just like every year. You are a gentleman, Mr. Corporal, I must say." She stood back and watched as Randolph managed the steps. Without the help of a railing, she noted. Good for him. Grit, she thought.

Randolph concentrated as he approached the door. No use lettin' this woman know my feelings, he decided, no matter how nice she thinks she's being.

"Happy New Year, Mrs. Aylesforth. And a black-haired man the first to visit you." Randolph smiled, and was a bit surprised to realize that it was sincere.

"Come in. Let us visit for a bit. I'd like to talk to you, see how you're faring." Helen backed out of the vestibule, indicated that they should go to the front room. She had set out two small glasses and a whiskey decanter. A plate of fruitcake sat in the middle of the side table.

"Let us celebrate a new year. Last year's well behind us, don't you agree?" Helen poured a finger's worth of bourbon into two glasses. Randolph laid his crutches by his chair, sat straight. He was not prepared for a visit, or more likely a lecture, from the owner of the big house. She was interfering too much in their lives, he thought. All right for Myrtle; she liked it that way. Even Arbutus, who had lost her usual sarcasm when it came to whom she now referred to as her "benefactor." And as he reviewed his thoughts, he also realized how much she had done for him, helped him in his recovery, made sure his family was taken care of. Still, she treats us all like children, he said to himself, like we can't think, or do, for ourselves.

He sat, still wearing his coat. Helen sensed his discomfort, attempted to put him a bit more at ease.

"You are getting along just fine with those crutches, Randolph. I know that it isn't easy.

"This whole year has not been easy for you. And it is good that you've spent your time working on your recovery. We must think of your future. You are still a young man, and you have much to offer. Your condition, well, we must admit that it limits your prospects.

"But you cannot spend your time in that house. Too many women there. You need to have some type of employment. You need that, for yourself, as well as your family. I have been thinking about that. I don't have a solution yet, but I wanted you to know that I have not forgotten you.

"Let us drink to a year of prospects."

Here I am, sitting in this rich old woman's house, drinking her whiskey, Randolph thought, as he raised the glass to his lips. And the taste brought memories of New Year's Eve a year ago, a long year ago. Helen Aylesforth's voice brought him back to the present.

"Well, you and your family have a good day. Tell Myrtle that she need not come this afternoon. I will be just fine on my own. You take the day for yourselves." She went to the sideboard where a fifth of whiskey sat.

"Happy New Year," she said. "A good whiskey for you and a wish for triumph over adversity."

Randolph thanked her, happy to return to his family. Now she's planning my life, he thought as he maneuvered his way to the alley, the bottle stuffed in his right pocket. He was both grateful and annoyed.

She means well, he thought. He thought of Myrtle, so sure that Miss Helen knew it all, that she had to listen to her, had to do what she said. Arbutus, too. That woman has too much power over us. I am the man of the family; they should respect me, not some old white woman tellin' everybody what to do, like she's some kind of queen or something.

Yet here they were, living in her house. He and Arbutus knew that their home belonged to Miss Helen, though Myrtle spoke and thought of it as her own. Yeah, Randolph thought, until they want you gone. Then you'll be out of there in the time it takes to pack up your dishes and corn meal. Myrtle doesn't see it, not at all. Arbutus, well, she understands, but she's grateful, obliged, indebted to her for every single favor that that woman bestows. She's no different from Myrtle, thinks that old woman knows everything.

Randolph banged his right crutch against the frozen ground. It's like she thinks Arbutus is her daughter, lookin' out for her, givin' her advice. Her own daughter, that Cantata woman, she don't mean much to her, she don't count for much in that house.

Well, he thought as he righted himself after a skid on a sliver of ice in the yard, I've got way too many worries of my own to take on some rich white woman's. More than enough.

No matter; I know what's important today. The New Year. A new year. And here I am, one leg and two fingers down. But I got a good bottle and Arbutus waiting for me at least.

January 10, 1914

———◇———

Hollins Street

Helen Aylesforth descended the stairway with a spring in her step. It surprised her, and she decided that she liked it. She called to Myrtle as she placed the heavy ivory-colored envelope on the telephone table in the hallway.

"Come, Myrtle, let us have our morning coffee together. I have something that I'd like to discuss with you."

Myrtle came to the kitchen stairs. "I'll be right up, Miss Helen. Just putting the dinner dishes in to soak." Myrtle ascended the stairs, this morning slower than usual.

By the time she arrived, Helen had arranged the cups, saucers, and breakfast plates, and had placed a pastry in front of Myrtle's place.

"A bit of a celebration this morning, Myrtle. It came to me in the night.

"Randolph, what he can do with his life. Cigars, Myrtle. Cigars! A perfect solution. As soon as we finish our breakfast I would like you to take my note to Mrs. Ellis one block down. You know where she lives. Mr. Ellis owns a cigar manufacturing business. I will see to it that Randolph has a job. Now what do you think of that! It is my intention to have this problem solved by evening. There is always a solution if one just works hard enough.

"I must admit that this was a difficult nut to crack. And the answer just came to me in the night. I told Randolph that I would find a solution. And here it is. Myrtle, this is a good day."

Myrtle added sugar, three teaspoons, to her coffee, stirred it without speaking. As she reached for the creamer, she said, "Miss Helen, thank you. You always savin' our family, doin' what's best for us." She added the cream, pulling the pitcher upright when the white reached the top of the coffee. "I'm sure Randolph will be grateful when I tell him. But maybe it be best to wait until you have it all worked out. I wouldn't want to get his hopes up and then have it not work out."

"Nonsense. Of course it will work out. I'll see to that. But you may be right. Perhaps it is best to wait. Until I get the details worked out."

Helen sat back in her chair, allowed her back to slump.

"I was looking out at the back yard this morning, at those two old lilac trees. So old they've grown together now; you can only tell that there are two of them in the winter when their leaves have fallen. Do you remember, Myrtle? That time we climbed them? And got so high that we broke those two branches with our weight? Wasn't that a time?"

Helen laughed so hard that her shoulders shook. Myrtle reached over to take her hand. "Oh, I remember all right. And Mammy whooped me so that I couldn't sit for days. Said I had led you down the path to sin."

Helen removed her handkerchief from her pocket, wiped her eyes and handed it to Myrtle. "Oh, Myrtle. Isn't that right? And it was I who made you climb with me. Do you remember that? I told Mama that I was the one, but your mother wouldn't listen.

"You've been quite the friend to me, all these years. You are my oldest friend, Myrtle; I trust you with my life."

"Lots of years, Miss Helen, lots that we been through together."

Helen straightened, sat back, her hands flat on the table. "And now, we fix Randolph."

An hour later, Myrtle returned from the Ellis house with an invitation for Helen to visit, that afternoon or the next day. No use waiting Helen thought, and returned to her room to dress – a grey wool suit, only a few years old, new to her, with black soutache trim. One of Arbutus's creations.

An easy visit with Margaret Ellis, an old acquaintance. Both women respected the other; both were quiet, without pretention, or so they thought.

Margaret knew of Randolph's situation, assured Helen that her husband would understand, that he could always use another responsible employee. She would telephone that evening, after she talked with him, after dinner.

January 11, 1914

The Alley, Hollins Street

Randolph stood in the middle of the kitchen, leaned on his crutch. "I ain't workin' in no cigar factory, Miss Myrtle. She can't do that to me. She just went out and did that and never even talked to me. How could you let her do that? How could you just let her think that she controls my life so much that she can tell me where to work and what I'll be doin'?

"A cigar factory? Inside a building all day? I may only have one leg, but I got to breathe the air. I been cooped up in this house all these months, but at least I can go outside, walk the streets if I feel like it. What would I do in one of those factories, no air, no windows, just tobacco? I'm not doin' it. I'm not. I'm goin' over there right now and tellin' that old woman just what I think of her and her plans, her plans for us, like we can't get by without her."

Arbutus sat at the table, listening to Randolph fume, glad that the children were in school. When he took a breath, she pulled out the chair to her right.

"Randolph, let's sit here for a few minutes, think this through." She knew not to lecture, that it was best to wait until he calmed down before she talked to him, talked some sense into him.

Randolph sat beside her, propped the crutches by the door. Arbutus took his hand.

"We have to be reasonable about this. Work, any kind of work, that will be good for you, a start. If you can get this job, manage it, then if you don't like it, maybe you'll be able to find another sometime. But we can't pass up this chance.

"Oh, I know, Miss Helen, she acts like the boss, fixin' up everybody, everything. But sometimes, most times, it's for our own good. She just helps us get where we need to be. Maybe we can't get there on our own. She means well, she does.

"And the money, you'd be earning money. We need that, so that we won't always be so dependent on her. You know that."

Randolph brought his hands down on the table, hard. Arbutus flinched.

"I got money. Where's that money that's owed me from the accident? Where is that?"

Myrtle, who had been listening from the corner of the room, interrupted. "I done tol' you. No blood money is comin' into this house. I am the boss on that. No blood money. We have suffered enough. You brought all this on with your blasphemin'. You will not bring more misery here."

Randolph pushed himself to his feet, reached for his crutches and went into the yard. Arbutus followed him, put her arms around him.

"My sweet Randolph. Pay her no mind. She's an old woman, stuck on her Bible and what she thinks God thinks. She loves you, us, the children. And we got no other place to go. Come on in the house. Let's sit a while, then you go and talk to Miss Helen. She cares for you; I know she does."

Two days later Randolph started work at H. Ellis and Company, makers of fine cigars. Mr. Ellis knew about Randolph's accident and the loss of his leg. He didn't know that Randolph was missing two fingers on his right hand. But he had given his word, and directed the foreman to devise a way that a three-fingered worker could roll a cigar.

Randolph was assigned to the department making *The Recruits*, thin cigars that came five or ten to a box, and to his surprise, he found that he soon came to enjoy the rhythm of his work, having his own space, his own tools. When the men joked that he needed to be careful with the trimmer, "to make sure you keep those fingers you still got," he laughed right along with them. He liked being with men again, away from all those women in his house. He began to hum some ragtime. The men liked what they heard, and some sang along with him.

The foreman noticed. Randolph did a workmanlike job. He was satisfied. The new fellow fit in, he told Mr. Ellis, who let out a slight sigh of relief.

March 8, 1914

Hollins Street

Myrtle was buttoning the third button of her winter coat, the one that Mrs. Aylesforth had passed on to her a decade ago and Arbutus had hemmed, when she heard her employer enter the back room.

"Send Lillian over to see me. I haven't seen her in, well, I can't remember the last time she was here. I want to make sure that she's keeping up with her reading. I know that Wanderer helps her, and passes on some of his books, the ones he thinks she'll like. And Arbutus, she says that, well, I haven't asked her recently. So, yes, you send Lillian over. Today or tomorrow, either one. That will be fine. I'll go through some of Cantata's old books, see if there are any that Lillian might like."

Myrtle nodded. "That be good of you, Miss Helen." And she turned to go to her home.

As she walked the short distance, she shook her head. Oh, Laws, she thought, poor little Lillian Gish. Having to stand before Miss Helen, recite, maybe even read for her. I'll have to drag her there, fightin' me every step.

Randolph shook his head when he heard. "Miss Myrtle, such news at the dinner table. Makes a rice pudding necessary to get over it." He turned to his daughter. "A royal command, baby. You gots to go. No use moanin' over it. Like a toothache. Get it pulled and get it over with. No use cryin' and whinin'."

Arbutus frowned at Randolph. "Now don't go making her feel bad" She turned to her daughter. "Lillian Gish, Miss Helen just wants to make sure that you are progressing. She has your best interests at heart."

Wanderer interrupted. "I'll go with her, Pops. Maybe Miss Helen has more books for me. I can tell her about the ones I've read. She promised me more whenever I want them."

Myrtle sat, listening to the chatter. When she saw that the family was concentrating on the pudding, she said, "Miss Helen asked to see Lillian Gish, and that's who she wants to see. And that's who she'll see." She looked over at her granddaughter, who was pushed so close to Camelia that they occupied the same chair. "Tomorrow, after school, just knock on the back door. I'll be there; I'll be with you. Ain't nothin' to be scared of, child. That woman wants to be sure that you are educated. Don't do nothin' that would make her not want that, you understand?"

Lillian Gish, who had remained silent throughout the meal, nodded, and leaned further into her aunt.

Two days later, Helen Aylesforth sat at the dining room table with Myrtle. "The child needs to see a dentist, Myrtle. She can't go through life with those teeth. She will never succeed. That is all people will see, and they will judge her for that. It doesn't matter what she does, or how intelligent she is, they will not give her a chance. How could this have slipped my notice? Why have you not said anything to me about this? This is an important aspect of her life. I cannot believe that neither you nor Arbutus has brought this to my attention."

She paused. "I must say that I am disappointed in you, Myrtle. I had hoped that you knew how much the lives of those children mean to me, that they be successful. Those teeth. No, never with those teeth.

"She must see a dentist immediately. I will arrange it and let you know. Now, do I need to speak to Arbutus, or can you relay my feelings to her? This is a matter of great importance. I will figure this out; we will make this right."

A week later, Lillian Gish, who was told that it was all right to miss school that day, and dressed in last year's Easter dress and shoes, both now one size too small, was delivered to the back door of the big house. Helen Aylesforth was waiting for her.

"You look quite nice in that outfit, Lillian. And you will look better after we visit the dentist. Not, mind you, that you should concentrate on beauty. No, you must develop your mind. But, still, yes, you will look better. There is nothing wrong in saying that, or in believing that, as long as you realize that it is your mind, your intelligence, that is the most important thing in life. I'm sure that your mother and your grandmother have emphasized that. And your brother. Emulate him, Lillian. It is a good thing to do that." She reached for the child's hand. Lillian Gish pushed up against her grandmother. Myrtle pushed her forward, leaned down, whispered what she hoped were soothing words.

"Can't you come, Gramam? You come?"

Helen Aylesforth stepped back, thought before she spoke. "I know it is a new journey for you. That is always frightening. Yes, for all of us, whether we are children or not. But, Lillian, I will be with you. This is something that you must do. You must be strong, and brave, and you will see how proud of yourself you will be on the journey home.

She turned toward Myrtle. "Are they selling ice cream at the market today? Perhaps while we are busy downtown, you could purchase some. Then we could have it when we get home, even ask Wanderer if you'd like. Lillian, if you would like it to be just the three of us, that would be fine too. You can be thinking about it while you meet the dentist.

"He's going to have a look at your teeth, make them straighter. You won't have to put your hand in front of your mouth all the time then. Your teeth will be big and white and perfectly straight. Like Wanderer's. You'll see, Lillian. Everything will be fine."

She saw that the child's eyes were red-rimmed. "Myrtle, tell the child. Make her understand. See that she is no longer afraid."

Helen had called John Abbott. Since that drive to the docks a year ago, she had counted on him to drive her where she needed to go. Easier that way, she thought. He knew what to expect. She didn't need to assert her authority. Sometimes it took so much effort, she admitted to herself. Sometimes, she thought, I'm just so tired.

Abbott waited at the curb for his fare. By this time, he didn't raise an eyebrow when Mrs. Aylesforth came down the front steps escorting a gangly colored girl. She's always doing something crazy, he thought, as he helped them into the back seat. Helen gave him the address -- downtown, Baltimore Street.

"I anticipate that we will be no longer than one hour, John. It would do good for you to be waiting after forty minutes. That meets with your schedule and approval, I assume?"

He nodded. No use arguing, no use explaining that every minute he waited was a potential fare wasted. She was an adequate tipper, but was not overly generous, although he was sure that she considered herself bountiful. These rich bitches, he thought. Not a care in the world; they all think that everyone exists just to serve them. And most times they're right. Shit, he thought. Shit. But what can you do?

Dr. Gatch's second-floor office was at the top of a narrow, dark stairway. Lillian Gish noticed the gold lettering on the opaque glass door. *Frederick W. Gatch, Dentist.* She wished she had a hand to hold, wished that Miss Helen would reach down and touch her hand, wished for a pat on the head. None came.

Instead, Lillian Gish heard gasps from the three women in the waiting room, saw them pull their pocketbooks closer to their bodies, felt their surprise and disapproval, though they said nothing.

Mrs. Aylesforth went directly to the secretary's desk to the right of the door. "Dr. Gatch is expecting us, I believe." She said this loudly and with what she deemed an air of authority.

The secretary's eyes widened, although she said nothing. The women in the waiting room looked at one another, though they too were silent.

"Lillian, let us sit by the window," Mrs. Aylesforth said, steering the child to the far corner of the room.

The two newcomers sat, hands folded in their laps as one of the woman rose, went to the desk. "I believe that there is a problem. We are not in the habit of waiting in a room with coloreds. Surely Dr. Gatch does not treat Negroes. You must ask these people to leave."

Helen observed the interchange, then cleared her throat. She considered walking to the desk, then decided against it. Instead, sure that her voice would be heard throughout the room, she addressed the secretary.

"There is no problem here, is there? I spoke with Dr. Gatch, told him that I was bringing the daughter of an associate. An associate, I might add, who does not wish to be insulted by anyone who might be in this waiting room."

The woman turned to Helen, then turned back to the secretary. "Get Dr. Gatch. I will not be treated in this manner. And I will not be exposed to waiting with coloreds. Do you understand me? You tell Dr. Gatch that should he accept this Negro, he will have no patients. I will see to that."

At this, Helen Aylesforth stood, walked to the desk, faced the woman. "I suggest then that you find another dentist.

"I will not ask you for an apology. I understand that this is an unusual situation. I will ascribe your lack of manners to that. I suggest that you return to your home and think about what you have done."

The two other patients watched in silence. Helen noticed that the secretary was crying, and behind her she heard Lillian's sniffles. She nodded to the group and returned to her seat. Leaning close to Lillian Gish, she said, "Child, you will have much to face. Keep your tears until you are alone. When you are with others, maintain your composure." She extracted a white linen handkerchief from her pocketbook and handed it to Lillian.

"Wipe your face, and look people in the eye. Straight in the eye. Not haughty, do you know that word? Not with distain, but with faith in yourself. And you can keep the handkerchief. Never leave the house without one."

The dentist stood, legs apart, when the two entered his office. He folded his hands in front of him.

"Mrs. Aylesforth, this is not what you led me to understand. You did not present the, uh," he struggled for words, "the situation clearly. Certainly we cannot have this. I must ask you to leave."

Helen Aylesforth did not leave. Rather, by the end of the session, during which Lillian Gish had braces applied, she and Dr. Gatch had concluded an arrangement where Mrs. Aylesforth would accompany Lillian Gish to her appointments, an hour after close of business. For this compromise, Dr. Gatch received payment thirty percent higher than his normal fee. "For extenuating circumstances," as they both agreed.

When the two left the dentist's office ninety minutes later, as expected, John was waiting at the curb. "Home, please. We have had a rigorous morning."

Lillian Gish struggled not to sniffle, but kept the handkerchief to her face. Her teeth, her mouth, her head ached. When they arrived at Hollins Street, Arbutus and Myrtle met them.

Helen did the talking. Lillian Gish stood in the doorway This time she didn't run to her family. "Ice cream," came her whispered request, and the four gathered round the table. Vanilla. It felt cool against the bands on her teeth.

While they ate, Helen gave the group their instructions. "She has a mouth full of metal and rubber bands. You can rub her gums with whiskey every few hours for the first few days. And replace the rubber bands every day. She may remove them for meals. Best not to draw attention to it."

The metal cut her mouth. The whiskey they gave her burned. But it got better, or she got used to it. But mostly, she wanted to be at home, with Melie.

Still she said nothing at school, for now the boys who called her "Buck Teeth," had an added epithet. No one at the school had ever seen anyone in braces, not even on the children of the white families their parents worked for. She listened, and read, and knew that she knew more than those who taunted her. Not as smart as Wanderer, though, and she knew that Wanderer didn't need to be smart. He had personality, that's what Gramam said. She said that's all he needed to get by in the world. She said that being smart on top it, well, for Wanderer the world was his oyster. That's what she said.

But for Lillian Gish, what she wanted most was to be at home, with Melie.

April 17, 1914

Hollins Street

Helen descended the stairs with a purpose. Standing by the phone table, she opened the navy blue leather address book to "L." She ran her finger down the page until she reached "Raymond Stroemeyer, lawyer" then turned to check the time shown on the green ormolu clock on the mantle in the front room. Surely he would be there at 8:20, she thought.

The phone was answered on the second ring. "Put me through to Mr. Stroemeyer. This is Helen Aylesforth." Within seconds, a male voice greeted his client.

"Raymond, I am in need of some assistance and think that you can be of help. I am seeking to rent a studio space for an associate of mine. We are looking for a downtown site, a second floor would be fine, in fact, it would be preferable, a location easily accessible by motor car, and, perhaps, streetcars as well. A bright space, sunlight, appropriate sanitary facilities, of course." She paused.

"My associate is a *modiste*."

"Mrs. Aylesforth, what is a *modiste?*"

Helen closed her eyes. "She designs, she makes, clothes, dresses," she responded, making no effort to hide her irritation and impatience.

Stroemeyer smiled to himself. "Ah, I see. That information will help in my search. And you would like us to locate, to recommend, one or two locations"

"Yes. Of course, I will want to visit them and make the final decision."

"Mrs. Aylesforth, am I to understand that this studio is for you?"

Helen shook her head as she answered. "Oh no, not in the least. I've told you that. It is for a very talented associate. I am merely acting as her," Helen hesitated, "her, ah, benefactor. Well, that is not quite the correct term."

Stroemeyer had never experienced his client at a loss for words.

"Mrs. Aylesforth, give us a few days. We will be in touch as soon as we find something suitable."

Smiling as she replaced the earpiece, Helen walked toward the dining room. She called to Myrtle.

"Let me tell you what is underway."

The following Thursday morning, at the stroke of nine, Helen went to the front door. John Abbot waited at the curb.

"You are a godsend, my dear fellow," she said as he helped her into the back seat of his cab. "I hope to negotiate a real estate transaction this morning. I've not done anything like it before, and I am a bit uneasy." Helen was surprised to confide such feelings, to a tradesman, and a stranger at that. But she also realized that it felt agreeable, a relief. What, after all, could be the harm, she asked herself, as she gave him the address on Eutaw Street.

Here she is on another of her adventures, Abbott thought. And she will expect me to wait for her. He pictured a series of lost fares as he drove her to her destination.

The cab stopped in front of a building that housed a milliner. Hats, Helen thought, hats. Just the thing! A milliner and a *modiste*. Perfect. She smiled at her luck, then realized that it was actually Arbutus's luck. No matter. Luck. Take it wherever you find it, she thought, and was surprised that she felt so delighted.

"Mr. Abbott, would you accompany me to the second floor? That is where I am to meet with the building's owner. I would prefer not to wait alone, in case I've arrived before he."

Abbott nodded and left his seat to help his fare from the car. Now I am her chauffeur, he thought. Rich bitch. But he held her arm gently as he escorted her into the building.

August Strauff was waiting at the entrance to the second floor doorway. Helen extended her hand to him. Abbott knew that he was dismissed and returned to his car, wondering what it was about this woman that made him stay with her.

Helen entered the large room, empty, but spotlessly cleaned. "You do a good job keeping the building up," she said. August noted that her gloved hand wiped the window as she looked out onto Eutaw Street.

She turned to face him, clasped her hands at her waist. "I will come to the point, Mr. Strauff. I am interested in this space for my associate. She is a *modiste* of the finest order, and has many valued customers. I think that her business, and the millinery below, will serve to complement one another. It will be a good partnership, so to speak, and a wise business decision on your part."

August watched and listened, interested to know when he would learn the twist in this story. Why was this woman, obviously well-bred, coming to do the footwork of her "associate"? He cleared his throat, waiting for her to come to the point.

When she remained silent, he said, "Yes. I am pleased that you like the space. It is a well-run building, and the first-floor tenant is of impeccable character."

"Yes," Helen answered, deciding that it was the right time to tell August about Arbutus, and hoping that the right words would come to her.

"I will come directly to the point, Mr. Strauff. My associate, Arbutus Corporal, is a Negress. A Negress of the finest order, I might add. I have known her and her family since she was born, and am prepared to vouch for their integrity and honor."

August stepped back as he heard Helen's words. This was not among the alternatives he had considered. "*Ach*," he muttered, allowing a German word to escape before he stopped himself. "Ah," he corrected himself, "Mrs. Aylesforth, this is not something that I have considered. I will have to deliberate about such an action. This is not something that I can agree to without much thought."

"Mr. Strauff, I can see that you are a man of the world. Surely you know that the finest *modistes* in Paris are of African origin. And the backbone, the foundation, of many, at least two, of the Washington fashion houses, are Negroes, though they use the names of white designers.

"My associate has developed a sizable circle of clients, all white, I might add. There is no deception there, none at all. Your allowing her to rent a studio in your building, that would bring these customers to your building, I believe they term it 'the carriage trade.'" Helen saw that she had touched a spark in her potential landlord, or, rather, she corrected herself, Arbutus's potential landlord.

"You have obviously accomplished a great deal in your life. I am familiar with your background, and it is most commendable, sir. This would be an opportunity to enhance your reputation, to step forward with an admirable action."

August Strauff touched his mustache, adjusted his monocle, quite aware of Helen Aylesforth's motives. Still, he liked this woman, liked that she had called him "sir." So sure of herself, her causes, she reminded him of Clara.

Ah, Clara, he thought. Perhaps this *modiste* could persuade his daughter out of her somber blacks and brown wardrobe, add a bit of vivacity to her appearance.

Thirty minutes later, an agreement had been struck, a year's lease, six months' rent paid in advance. Helen would supply wallpaper and a brass stair railing; August would pay for installation and mount a sign that would hang from the building:

Arbutus Corporal,
Modiste
Dressmaker

the latter suggested by August who gently proposed that Mrs. Corporal may want to attract customers who were not yet familiar with the French term.

Helen, initially offended by such a recommendation, and from the landlord at that, hesitated, then agreed. August Strauff, a good man to listen to, she thought, good ideas.

The pair descended the steep stairs to the street. They shook hands, both satisfied that they had struck a fair deal.

Abbott stood by the cab and helped his fare into the back seat. Helen Aylesforth smiled. A good day's work, she thought.

For the next weeks, the house on Hollins Street was filled with activity. Helen woke to the whirr of the sewing machine from the back room on the second floor. Fabric swatches arrived each day with the morning's post. Arbutus descended to the first floor only when Helen insisted that she stop for lunch and an afternoon tea. Myrtle bustled in the kitchen, dusted the furniture with a new spirit. "Like the old days, Miss Helen, all this bustlin' around. Jes' like the old days."

Helen smiled. Myrtle was right. She had forgotten the heady feeling of being occupied, taken up with a cause, a task outside herself. She busied herself making lists, making plans for the shop, making plans to be sure that the business succeeded. At the dining room table each noon, she reviewed her notes with Arbutus.

"Now make sure that you have enough samples to please different types of customers. I know that you like those new styles, draped, soft, but many of your older customers aren't going to wear, or buy, them. You don't want them to feel put off when they come to the shop. So be sure to have some of the more conservative dresses out where they can be seen. And dress forms, at least two, perhaps three. You'll need one or two as you work on costumes for your customers, but I think it would be a nice touch to have one completely outfitted. So that they can see the finished quality of your work. Yes. I'll work on getting those." Helen added to her list.

"You'll make appointments most times, so you can fix up the area to suit your client. That's right, I think it would be best to refer to them as clients rather than customers. You don't want them to think you're a department store, with ready-to-wear. No, these will be custom-made, custom-fitted."

Helen didn't give Arbutus a chance to respond. She consulted the list she had made that morning.

"Now, I think it would be a good idea to place a discrete advertisement in the *Baltimore Sun*. I can take care of that for you, so you can concentrate on getting the sample costumes ready to move to Eutaw Street. And boxes, we can order the best quality boxes, I think. White, with **Arbutus Corporal**, *modiste*, engraved, not printed, on the box. And then wide satin ribbons to tie around it.

"Yes, we must think of colors. What we want to have as a theme, so that when people see them, they will think of you. So, you can give that some thought. I think that, as long as they are tasteful, any ones will do. So, the boxes will be a creamy white, and then the ribbon color you can choose and let me know. Tomorrow. I will order from my stationer. They'll know exactly what to do.

"And the furnishings. The wallpaper hanger will come by with samples by week's end. I think that we should choose that first, and then fill in. You won't need a lot, just a few nice chairs and a comfortable sofa. And a screen, of course, a silk screen. Heavens, I didn't realize there were so many details to opening up just a business like this."

Myrtle stood at the head of the table and watched the two. Arbutus has never looked prettier, she thought. And Miss Helen, she looks years younger. And she's actually eating, cleaning her plate. It had been a long time since Myrtle had seen that.

What Myrtle had taken for a blush on Arbutus's face was the flush of nervousness. Helen was talking too fast, making too many plans. It felt out of control to Arbutus. Something did not sit quite right. Miss Helen making all these plans. But it is my business, Arbutus thought. But all these details, boxes, ribbons, calling cards, even a telephone. So many details, so many expenses. And the only thing I know how to do is sew.

That afternoon, Arbutus did not join the women for tea. She told her mother that she needed to finish an outfit before she left that evening. Arbutus closed the door and stood by the window. Looking out on the street, she saw the lamplighter making his rounds.

I don't know why I'm doing all this, she said to herself, half aloud. I don't know anything about having a shop. I know how to sew; I know how to make up patterns. I know how to put colors and fabric together so that the dresses turn out lovely. But I don't want to have to know about boxes, and calling cards, and advertising in the papers. I don't know what this is all about. And Miss Helen is just taking over and bossing, bossing, bossing. She's the one having the good time. I'm just up here sewing. And now I have a shop with six months' rent paid.

She put her head against the glass. The cool calmed her. Gradually her heartbeat slowed. She raised her head, put her hand up to adjust the ribbon in her hair. I just need to learn, she thought. I can do that.

April 29, 1914

Hollins Street

Every light in the Hollins Street house was lit that morning. Helen was dressed and had fixed her own tea when Myrtle arrived at 7:30 a.m. "No time to waste this morning, Myrtle. I'm thinking that the rain will stop soon. This will be a good day for all of us. Arbutus moving into her shop. The wallpaper is hung, the railing installed, and Mr. Strauff promised that her sign will be in place and waiting for us when we arrive."

Myrtle smiled and set the table for breakfast. "We all need a heavy breakfast this morning. Prepare us for the day ahead." She loved seeing her employer busy, happy, like the old Miss Helen, she thought.

Arbutus had shooed the children out the door by seven. It wouldn't hurt them to get to school early, she decided, for she wanted a few minutes alone with Randolph. He had been conspicuously quiet these past weeks, really months. She knew he was content with his job, had made friends, smiled more than he had in a long time. But she also sensed that he was keeping something inside, and that it had to do with her and the business.

He stood by the door, holding the lunch Myrtle had prepared. Arbutus, dressed for her day ahead, went to him, took his hand. "We been through so much, especially you. Now you have a job you like, and it is the start of a little business for me. Something that we can do, something we can do for the children, for ourselves. A new beginning, for both of us."

Randolph brought her hand to his lips. "You always the big boss, 'Butus. So now you have a real chance to run your own show. I'm just a workin' man, and grateful, lucky, to be that. You the big shot in the family." He paused, then smiled at her. "But you know who the man is, right? Who makes you, who gives you all that oomph you got?"

Arbutus pushed against him, gently enough to be sure that he didn't stumble. She kissed the side of his neck "You sure my man. That is one thing I know."

Randolph turned and headed east on the alley. Arbutus closed the door. He's right, she thought. I am the big shot in the family.

She gathered her wrap and headed to the big house.

When she arrived, she saw boxes of garments stacked in the front hallway. Helen turned to her. "Oh, you are just in time. We brought down all your samples. Abbott can carry your sewing machines and tools. He'll need to get a truck, a small one, to move the sofa and chairs. He can do that this afternoon while we're setting things up."

Arbutus started when Helen reached for her. Her employer, or rather, her benefactor was not one for physical contact. "This is a star-spangled day for us, Arbutus, for you. A star-spangled day!"

Abbott arrived, just as he had promised. Now she has me moving furniture, he thought, and smiled to himself. Each time she came up with another outrageous request, he complied, and then wondered why. There is just something about her, he thought. Just something about her.

When she told him he needed a truck, a small one, she said, to move even more furniture, he protested. At last, he said to himself, she has gone too far. Her response was to look at him quizzically, and ask, "Then how do you propose that we get the furniture where it needs to be?" He borrowed a truck, a small one, that afternoon.

At day's end, furniture in place, truck returned to rightful owner, the four workers surveyed their work. Abbott thought that it looked like a place where fine ladies would feel comfortable. Arbutus wondered if she would ever feel at home there, if she would ever feel that she belonged, would ever feel that this was hers. Myrtle took it all in. Her own flesh and blood, having such a fancy business, with such elegant, rich customers. What would Joshua have thought. She saw him smiling, so proud that his chest looked like it would burst.

And Helen looked around. Yes, just as it is supposed to be.

She turned to the group. "We have done ourselves proud, I think. And we deserve a good treat. Mr. Abbott, let us stop at Hopper McGaw and fill up a few baskets for our supper this evening. You will be able to share it with us, I hope."

When Abbott nodded, she gathered her things. "Mr. Abbott, Myrtle, I'd like a few minutes with Arbutus. We will see you downstairs at the car." The two knew that they were dismissed and turned to leave the shop.

Helen turned to Arbutus. "I have a little gift for you, well, for the business." She reached into her carpetbag and withdrew a sturdy wooden box. "This is your cashbox. It belonged to Dr. James, and he had a very good sense about money. I think it is fitting that you have it now."

As Arbutus reached for it, Helen held onto it as well. "And a few words about money. You may think that I have no thoughts about money, but you would be wrong there. Money is very important, or at least *enough* money is very important. And now you will be in a position to earn money of your own." She paused, and Arbutus sensed her uncertainly about continuing. Arbutus had never seen her benefactor uncertain.

"I want to give you some advice. Always keep some money for yourself. No one has to know about it, but it should be your money and yours alone. Do you understand? It is money that only you know about. That is important. It will keep you safe, give you a feeling that you have some control about what happens to you.

"You may not understand now, but one day you will. Always keep some money that is just yours." She handed over the box.

Arbutus ran her hand over the smooth, varnished wood. "I know I should be saying thank you over and over again, Miss Helen. You have watched over us, and I don't know what we would have done without you. And you believed that I could do something. I will make this business a success. I want to pay you back for all that you have done, found this place for me, helped me get started."

Arbutus bit her lip, thought of Randolph, his thoughts about Helen running their lives. He was right, she knew, but today she was grateful.

The two women walked toward the stairway. "Do you have your keys, Arbutus?"

The younger woman grinned as she jingled the keys to her establishment.

Once in the car, Abbott made his way to Charles Street and Hopper

McGaw. The three waited while Helen put together their celebratory feast. When she returned to the car, as Abbott helped her into the back seat, she spoke to him. "Surely you will want to be with us for this. You are part of this undertaking, don't you think!"

Abbott nodded, but said nothing. Helen settled in, and found that she was smiling, widely. As the cab approached Hollins Street, she leaned toward Arbutus. "Wanderer. I want you to know that I have set funds aside for his education. No need to concern yourself about that."

August 20, 1914

Calvert Street

Nicholas sat at the dining room table, the front page of the *News Post* spread before him. Meg had poured his coffee and he heard her downstairs fixing his morning tray. He had early meetings in the office, clients nervous about the international state of affairs. He wished his father were there to advise him, for he knew that another mistake on his part would have dire consequences, for him and the company. He pushed his coffee aside and called down to Meg.

"Tea, please, Meg. You can bring it up with breakfast." Tea, he thought, that might settle my nerves. He took a deep breath, pulled his shoulders back. To look the part, he thought, to look in control, that is half the battle. He rattled the paper as he turned the page.

He felt a hand on his shoulder and turned to see his wife. "What in the world are you doing up at this hour? And downstairs? And dressed?"

Cantata smiled, and Nicolas realized that she was smiling more often these days.

"I wanted to get an early start on the day, and see you before you left for the office." She took the chair to his right. "I know this is a difficult time for you. Do you think that you'll hear from your father today? He'll know what the situation in Germany, in Europe is, much more than the papers. They always exaggerate things just to sell papers. He'll be able to give you guidance, don't you think? And he will be so proud of how you're handing this situation." She reached for his hand. "He should be, that is for sure. You are doing a wonderful job. I am proud of my import-ant husband." She leaned to kiss him on the cheek.

"I wish I had your confidence."

Meg appeared with tea and oatmeal. Surprised to see Cantata at the table, she asked for her breakfast order.

"I think eggs, bacon, toast, with jam, strawberry, and a pot of coffee. Don't forget the cream. And I heard the children up when I came downstairs. Best to get them ready for the day. I'll clear the table for you."

Nicholas rose to go.

Cantata looked up at him. Still handsome, she thought. "Today will be a good day for you. And your meetings will go splendidly. They will appreciate your guidance, Nicolas. And we can celebrate tonight, a special dinner. I'll speak to Meg."

***

St. Paul Place

When he arrived at the office, Johnston met him at the door. "A cablegram for you, Nicholas. It is on your desk.

Cablegram

August 20, 1914
Dresden, Germany
To: Nicholas Sherwood
        Chesapeake Casualty Insurance
        St. Paul Place
        Baltimore Maryland
        USA

War out of nowhere. German ships blockaded. Plan to England via Switzerland. Travel difficult, but all say war over by winter. Will send letter re business matters from Zurich.
Carry on. Do not worry.

Father

Nicholas held the yellow paper, smoothed it over with his right hand. Over by winter. Good news to relay to his clients. He smiled.

November 23, 1914

St. Paul Place

Nicholas studied the newspapers each morning, trying to make sense of the folly in Europe. Communication had all but stopped between the U.S. and Germany, and one never knew if letters and wires to France and England arrived. Most of the company's clients had curtailed operations to European ports.

Revenues were down; Nicholas was developing a plan to contact companies that traded exclusively in the Americas. He wished for his father's advice. He had heard nothing from him since his August cable.

As he sat at his desk that morning, Violet Marsh entered, a yellow envelop in her hand. She looked at Nicholas as she placed it before him.

Nicholas exhaled, and was surprised to hear the sound of his own breath. Finally, he thought, word from his father. He glanced up. "Thank you. Some word from my father, I am sure. It is a relief to all of us."

She nodded, and remained by his desk, hoping to be the first to learn what the cable said.

Nicholas looked up, waited for her to leave. When she made no move to do so, he said, "Thank you, Miss Marsh, for bringing this to me. It would be best if you returned to your work now."

Properly chastised, she nodded and left the office.

Cablegram

November 23, 1914
London, England
To: Nicholas Sherwood
        Chesapeake Casualty Insurance
        St. Paul Place
        Baltimore Maryland
        USA

Arrived London. With Susanna. Cable reply if letters have reached you. Things quite difficult here. Mines, torpedoes impede return. Will continue to write. Unsure if letters have reached you.
Carry on as best. Do not worry.

Father

***

Calvert Street

Cantata and Nicholas remained at the table after the dinner dishes had been cleared. Meg was in the basement; the children had been sent to their rooms to prepare for bed. Nicholas told Cantata of his father's cable. "I don't know what this means, for him, for us, for the business. Now they're saying that the war could go on for who knows how long. None of the companies are shipping to Europe, so our side of the business is almost dead. And I can't go to Father for his counsel."

Nicholas rubbed his forehead. "Cantata, I hate to bring this worry to you. You've been magnificent through this year, cutting back. And never complaining. I am so proud of you. Even the trouble with your mother. You've had all this, carried all this, on your own. And have been nothing but supportive to me." He leaned toward her to take her hand.

Cantata smiled. You have no idea, she thought, no idea. But she kept her feelings to herself. "You've done a brilliant job, especially with all that you've had on you, with no one to help you. When your father returns, he will see that. He could not have done better himself. I know that."

They sat without speaking. After a few moments, Cantata turned to him. "Nicholas, if the company has fewer clients, then that means that there is also less risk. Am I correct in thinking that?"

Nicholas looked at his wife, startled to hear her using such business terms.

"Well, it depends upon how you look at it, but, in a way, yes. Why in the world would such a thought come to you?"

Cantata folded her hands, placed them on the table. "And you do have reserves for those risks, yes? That is what you are repaying since the difficulty last year?"

Nicholas bit his lower lip, answered slowly. "Yes." He paused. "Why are you asking this?"

"It seems to me, though I do not have the head for business that you have, it seems to me that you have a cushion, so to speak, a cushion in those reserves. So, even if business is off a bit, for now, the company is still on sound financial footing." Cantata smiled and put her hand in front of her mouth. "Can you believe that I know those words? Sound financial footing?"

Nicholas bent his head. His wife was seducing him, he thought. And liked it.

"Perhaps we can continue our discussion upstairs," he suggested.

Cantata rose from her chair and took her husband's hand. As she led him up the stairs, she thought of the order that she'd place with Arbutus. A navy wool suit, with black soutache trim, a tea gown, grey chiffon, and a new evening dress for New Year's Eve, purple, a deep purple.

PART III
New Year's Eve, 1914

---◇---

St. Paul Place

Violet Marsh had notified the staff as Nicholas had directed, and they had gathered in the hallway outside his father's office. Nicholas ushered them in. He had rehearsed what he was about to say, wanted to be sure that he sounded assured, in control, like his father, like his father would have wanted.

Some were apprehensive, those who were aware of the decrease in business in the last months. Others wanted to get this speech over with so that they could start their holiday a few hours early.

Nicholas stood in front of his father's desk, cleared his throat, and began.

"This has been a most difficult few years for us. I'm sure that you are aware of that. We are a small business and we all work closely together. My father's extended absence was not anticipated, but I am proud to say that each one of you rose to the occasion."

Hearing his words, Nicholas worried that he sounded pompous, realized that he was attempting to parrot both his father's words and style. He feared that his audience knew that he was play-acting. As, he said to himself, he was.

He stopped, swallowed, and resolved to speak from his heart. It couldn't be any worse that what I've been doing, he decided. He cleared his throat, spread his fingers on his father's desk.

"All of you know that I am not my father. I don't have his experience; I don't have his knowledge of the clients. This war, for us it came out of nowhere. And for our clients as well. You know that our book of business has dwindled with the embargoes and dangers in Europe. But that is temporary. Our clients are seeking new markets, and they are finding them in Asia and South America. We will be there to insure them, as we have in the past. They trust us; they know that we are good for our word.

"But there will be a lag time for us, as they put together the details of their arrangements. Most likely it will be months. We can weather that storm. We have strong reserves, and I am working diligently to approach potential new clients.

"The war in Europe will soon be over. It will take a while to get back to business as usual there, but in the meantime we will have those additional outlets. I say this with every confidence, while being most aware of the difficulties we face in the short-term.

"I am committing to you that each one of you has no worries about the security of your position here. We will see to that."

Nicholas paused. He recognized that people were listening to him, paying attention to what he was saying, that they believed him.

"That being said," he continued, "the company will have to endure some restrictions. To that end, we are unable to grant any end-of-year bonuses."

He stopped. The group was silent; no one moved; all remained staring at him.

"I know that this is a disappointment. However, the decision was made as a way to ensure that each employee would retain both his position and salary. I want to assure you that, once business returns, we will continue our practice of providing yearly bonuses to all our employees.

"You have been loyal; you have been steadfast. You do my father proud. For that I am grateful."

Nicholas surveyed the group. They remained silent, waiting to be dismissed.

"Thank you, again, for all that you've done. I wish you a very happy new year. Enjoy your holiday and we will see you on Monday."

Nicholas moved to shake the hands of those present, then returned to his office. He closed the door, went to the window, looked out on the alleyway, and sighed with relief. Earlier that day he had directed Johnston to make payment to the bank for the loan his father had taken the year before. He leaned on the windowsill and smiled as he clicked his heels.

Then he sat at his desk to make a list of potential clients to contact in 1915.

★★★

Hollins Street

Helen had told Myrtle to leave early. Another New Year's Eve where she had no plans, and she was both grateful and melancholy. "But don't forget to make sure that Randolph comes tomorrow. We must continue that tradition."

Myrtle nodded. "Oh, he'll be here. We wouldn't do without that. And we all need all the good luck we can find. I'm soaking black-eye peas now, start them on the stove this evenin'." She looked over at Helen, noticed that she had become thinner. That Cantata, she thought. She's missin' her. And Jimmy. Like I miss my John, and Daisy, and Leroy, and pray that James and Solomon are alive at least. But Joshua, especially Joshua. Because I don't talk about them, don't mean I don't miss them.

She moved closer to her employer. "Jes' another year for us, Miss Helen. Another long year for us. Not sure what the next will bring. Bears not thinkin' about most of the time."

Helen took Myrtle's hand. "You know, Myrtle, I think you may be right. Too much thinking, too much remembering. It does no good sometimes. Most of the time, perhaps."

She stepped back, clasped her hands in front of her. "But, you go on now. Your family awaits, and those peas need tending to. I'll see Randolph tomorrow. And you tell Wanderer to be sure that he keeps up with his reading. He can come by any time and take any of the books in the house. He's old enough now to choose for himself."

Myrtle walked to the back door, took her coat from the hook she had used for as long as she could remember. She turned. "Happy New Year, Miss Helen. A good year ahead for all of us." She hoped she was right.

★★★

Calvert Street

"Meg, could you come upstairs for a bit? I'd like to talk to you while we have a few quiet moments."

Meg was sitting at the kitchen table, thinking about how she would spend her day off. New Year's Day. She had so few friends left. Perhaps she would visit Mrs. Wells, see how her former employer was doing, how the family was faring. So different from her current position. But all these rich people have their own set of woes, she thought. All this worry about money. Like there is never enough.

She wants something, Meg mumbled. That would be the only reason she would ask to see me, to assign another task. "Be right there, Mrs. Sherwood." One of these days I'll look for another job; maybe this year coming. That's what I'll do.

Cantata was sitting at the head of the dining room table. When Meg appeared, she asked her to sit with her.

Cantata smiled, not quite a genuine one, but the best that she could muster.

"Meg, I want to thank you for all that you have done for us this past year. Both Mr. Sherwood and I are aware of the extra duties you've taken on, and we want you to know how much we appreciate it.

"This year has been a very difficult one for us. I'm sure that you know that, living in such close quarters with us. First with our financial setback, then with the situation with my in-laws and the questions about that. But we are hopeful that 1915 will be different, that we will have resources to hire additional help here who can relieve you of those extra burdens you have taken on."

Cantata took a breath. Meg had not moved, nor had her expression changed. Cantata waited for her to acknowledge what she had said. When no comment was made, Cantata continued. Meg harbored a hope that a raise in pay would be offered, then put that idea out of her head.

"So," Cantata continued, "Mr. Sherwood and I would like to give you something to acknowledge your help this year." Cantata smiled and pushed an envelope toward Meg.

Meg took it, but did not open it. "Thank you, Mrs. Sherwood. I have enjoyed my time here. And enjoy looking after the children. They are fine young people."

As she said this, Meg resolved to find new employment. She recognized that she could not stand this woman, though she wasn't sure exactly why.

Cantata stood, still smiling. "And Meg, could I ask you to come to my room in about twenty minutes or so. I'd like to be dressed before Mr. Sherwood arrives, and I'm going to need just a bit of help with my dress." She went to the stairway without waiting for a response.

You handled that well, she said to herself, and smiled as she entered her bedroom. Once there she went to the closet and pulled out the eglantine crepe and chiffon evening dress that Arbutus had designed and sewn. This will show them, she thought. This will say that we are back. Meg arrived to fasten the twenty-seven hooks that secured the back of the dress.

Cantata was sitting in the front room when she heard Nicholas come in the back door. She called to him, anticipating his reaction when he saw her. She was not disappointed.

"You look stunning," he said as he entered the room. "All ready for yet another entrance to the Maryland Club."

"All ready for us to make an entrance," she said, and patted the space next to her for him to sit with her. "Let's relax here for a few minutes before you go upstairs to change. We have lots of time. No need to be there early."

Nicholas sighed as he took his place next to her.

"How did you do?" she asked.

Nicholas leaned back. "I think it went well. I told them the truth, but then how could they not have already known, or at least sensed, it? But at least it's out in the open now. I don't think it would have been the way Father would have dealt with it. He was, is, always in control, and I think that they have more faith in him than they do in me. I'm sure that the gossip has gone round about what I did. So they probably are correct in their distrust of me and my abilities."

Cantata started to protest, but he held up his hand to silence her.

"No. It's true, and it's best to face the facts of the matter. Which is what I did today. Now it is up to me to make sure that the company stays solvent. And, until this war is ended, the only way I know how to do this is to court the shipping companies and assume that they know best what will keep their enterprises afloat." He chuckled at his phrase.

Cantata did not catch his attempt at humor. She turned to him. "So, with your father gone, or not available to direct the company, Nicholas, it is you who are the president. They should be grateful for that, and treat you with respect. You don't need to explain anything to them!"

He stood. "I think I'll go upstairs to change now. Incidentally, you do look especially fetching tonight. Especially."

Those at the Maryland Club, or most of them at least, agreed.

★★★

Hollins Street, The Alley

Randolph smelled the greens as he turned the corner. Miss Myrtle is at it, he thought. A good day for them, for us, he thought. This year, not a bad one. Better than I expected. He felt in his pocket for the pint of whiskey, now significantly lighter than it had been when he picked it up at noon.

Steam poured out the door as he opened it to see his mother-in-law at her familiar place in front of the stove. He heard Wanderer practicing a new tune on his harmonica, and when he put his head round the corner of the bedroom, he saw Lillian Gish sitting on the bed keeping time. Good the girl likes music, he thought. Good she smiles when she hears music.

When Wanderer saw his father, he continued to play, making the syncopation even more pronounced. "I'm getting' it, Pops. Almost as good as you with the rhythm. We can make a team, the both of us playin' these tunes. Tonight, Pops? Like you promised?"

Randolph walked into the room. "Hush, now. Don't let your grandmother hear you. She'll be all over us. I'll say something to your mother when she gets in, but just keep this quiet for now, right? That's how we'll get where we need to be on New Year's Eve. Leave it to me, but you keep mum." Randolph laughed. "You like that word? You keep mum?" And father and son laughed.

Lillian Gish heard them. She smiled, and then put her hand in front of her mouth.

Hours later, Arbutus pushed open the door. Randolph hopped up from his chair to greet her; Myrtle went to take her coat. "I hope they paid you lots of money for all that last-minute work," she said to her daughter.

Arbutus smiled. "That they did, Mama, that they did. I even took a taxicab home."

Randolph looked at his wife, her face flushed with the sudden heat of the house. She had been working long hours these past months. He had been jealous, resentful, angry at life. She hadn't noticed. Then Christmas came and there was her gift. So, he thought, how can I be angry? Good times for the family, and I'm not doing too bad. He smiled to himself. Getting' just like Miss Myrtle, all this philosophizin'.

The family gathered round the table for their New Year's Eve meal. Arbutus talked about her customers, how three of them had to have ensembles finished by this evening, even though they had not come to her until just before Christmas. "They said they'd pay whatever it cost, so I charged them double. They didn't know it, and they just paid me, in advance. Two of them came in today, one so late that her husband waited in the car while she put the dress on right in the shop. Had all her jewels already in place. I practically sewed her into it."

She pushed herself back from the table. "But now a few days of rest. I just locked up tonight and said I deserve a few days off, with my family." She turned toward Randolph. "How you likin' your Christmas gift, baby?"

Randolph's smile glinted off the kerosene lamp. "I'm lovin' it baby. Got just what I've always wanted. A gold tooth and some walkin'-around money. With you, what else could a colored man want?" He put his hands on his suspenders, and looked sideways at Wanderer.

"Now, baby, with this gold tooth, and with this night, I thought it be just the time for me and Wanderer to go and hear, to play, a little music. Just a few hours; we'll be home before there could be any trouble."

Myrtle cleared the dishes from the table and stood back to watch. Arbutus straightened her shoulders, thought before she spoke.

"I know that this night is important to you, for you to go and spend

111

an hour or two," Arbutus emphasized the last words with a stern look at Randolph, "but not Wanderer. He's too young. He doesn't know his way around those places, those people, and I don't want him to learn."

She paused. "So you go, but you leave Wanderer here, with us. Where he belongs."

When he heard his mother's words, Wanderer started to protest. He had his argument rehearsed, that he was a man, that it was a good thing to learn his way in the world with his father by his side, better than on his own.

But Randolph shook his head, a signal for Wanderer to be silent.

He reached for Arbutus's hand. The way was not to argue, that he knew.

"Now, 'Butus, I know how you feel, and I thought that you would say this. But you got to think, consider. Here's this boy, 'round nothin' but women just about all the hours of the day. He's almost a man, look how he's growed this year. You gots to let him out, get out on his own, learn how a man acts. You keep him like this an' he'll be all sissified. How you think he get along then? You let his father show him what it is to be a man, how to act, how to do.

"And music, 'Butus, he got music in him. That got to come out. So let it out where people know it, appreciate it, clap for it, maybe even pay for it.

"We just be gone a few hours. I promise, my word. We be home just about midnight. No use no one-legged gimp out that late anyway. He'll be lookin' out for me too. Show him how to be a man."

Arbutus put her chin in her hand. Looked up at Randolph. "You got a way with words, Randolph, gold tooth or none." She shook her head. "You go." She looked at Wanderer. "But you be back by fifteen minutes after midnight, you understand? If you want to leave this house again, that's the time you'll be inside tonight."

Wanderer nodded, trying to maintain a solemn look. But his smile broke through as wide as the sky.

New Year's Day, 1915

Hollins Street

Helen was downstairs and waiting for Randolph to appear. Keep up this tradition, must keep up traditions, she thought. She walked from room to room, waiting, touching each of the china figurines on the mantle, moving them an inch, then replacing them in their original positions. She had not laid out any sweets. Not this year, she thought, but then went down to the kitchen and brought up the tin of ginger cakes. She arranged a few on a plate and took it to the front room. No use his suffering on my account, she thought. He has enough worries; a ginger cake might help his spirits.

The doorbell rang as she placed the plate on the side table. Randolph's New Year's gift sat beside it.

As Helen opened the door, she said, as she had said for more years than she could remember, "Ah, a black-haired man to welcome in the new year." She smiled as she said these words, and noticed that it felt sincere.

"Come in and sit a bit, Randolph. Tell me how you are getting along."

Randolph managed his crutches with skill now, and followed her into the front room where he sat in a side chair. He knew to choose chairs with arms, chairs with firm seats and backs. He knew that he had to be polite; he knew what he had to say. But he wanted to return home to his family on this day.

"We are all getting along fine, Miss Helen. I do appreciate your help in getting me the job at Ellis's. And the help with Lillian Gish's teeth. And the help getting Arbutus started in business. It has been a good year for us. We all thank you." He hoped that would be enough and that she would soon hand him his whiskey.

"I am glad I could be of help, Randolph. You are a most deserving family. You have much to be proud of." Helen stopped. She could think of no more to say.

"And so, here is your New Year's gift," and she managed a smile as she handed him the bottle.

Randolph thanked her. Helen walked him to the front door.

"A very happy New Year to you and your family."

"And to you, Miss Helen. Thank you again." Randolph turned to maneuver down the front steps.

Helen started to push the door closed, then opened it and called to him. "And Wanderer, he is keeping up with his reading, is he not? He knows that he can come any time and take any book he'd like. He's made such progress; he can read anything now. A smart boy you have there, a very bright young man."

Randolph turned once he reached the sidewalk. "Oh, Wanderer, he reads all the time. We all know he the bright one in the family."

Helen watched as he went toward the back of the house. A good man, she thought. A good family.

She leaned against the staircase deciding what to do next. A nap, perhaps. And she took the stairs more slowly than she had in the past.

Once on the second floor, she turned toward James's study. She moved to his desk and opened the middle drawer. His pens, a few bottles of ink, remained, untouched since he last used them. She took one of the bottles, shook it, and removed the top. She unscrewed the cap of the black Waterman pen and dipped it into the ink, then scribbled a few lines on the paper on the desk. The pen, unused these many years, glided smoothly over the paper.

She sat for a few minutes, then decided. I'll call Stroemeyer tomorrow.

★★★

Hollins Street, The Alley

The family sat around the table. Myrtle stood by the stove, waiting for Randolph's return to start ladling out the New Year's dinner. Arbutus had been telling them about some of her customers, imitating the way some of them pointed to the fabrics they wanted, others depending on her advice. "I just get to know them and give them what they want. And they have so much money, they will never have enough." She shook her head. "Rich people, they don't know what they want, just that they want more, different." She shrugged. "Now I ain't sayin' that I wouldn't like more, different, but I think I'd know when it was enough."

"When what was enough?" Randolph heard her last words as he came in the door.

"Oh, you know. Rich people. They ain't no happier even with all that money. Look at Miss Helen, Miss Cantata."

Myrtle brought some plates to the table. "Now let's not go talkin' about Miss Helen on this day. Randolph, she give you that bottle? Maybe it's time that we all had a nip. Just for New Years, now. Just as a celebration."

"Mama! I don't believe what I just heard. You asking for a 'nip'?" Arbutus laughed, Wanderer banged his fork on the table, even Lillian Gish grinned and forgot to cover her mouth. Randolph broke the seal. "I would be delighted to give you a drink, Miss Myrtle. To celebrate the holiday. In fact, I think it would do for all of us to partake. Wanderer, Lillian Gish, you fill your glasses with water and I'll put just a drop on the top. Then we can all drink to 1915.

"Now if this ain't a New Year's Day to remember!"

As the family toasted themselves, Myrtle gave a silent toast, to Joshua.

That afternoon, dishes washed and put away, and the house redolent with the smell of ham hocks, the family sat around the kitchen stove, Melie knitting, Myrtle in the rocking chair, eyes closed, Arbutus looking through issues of *McCall's* and *The Delineator*. Randolph and Wanderer practiced a few rhythm sequences. Lillian Gish sat on the bed in the back room, watching, thinking.

Wanderer lay down his harmonica. "Mama, they all liked our music last night. One man said that I had real talent, that I was worth watching. Didn't he, Pops. Didn't he say that to me?"

Randolph shifted his banjo and shook his head slightly, a warning that Wanderer didn't see.

"And he said that there were opportunities for me, in Baltimore. That he could make opportunities available for me. He meant it, I think, didn't he, Pops?"

Arbutus had put down her magazines and watched her son and her husband.

"He said that he could get me a job at The Rennert. Can you believe it? The Rennert! That I could learn to be a waiter there. Just like Mr. Robert Foster. You know, he always wears those fancy suits, white shirts, shoes shined just so. He's a waiter. At The Rennert. There is no place fancier than that. Now I would have to learn, would have to start low, but he thinks I have the potential, that is the word he used, potential, to be a waiter there."

Arbutus stood, walked over to Randolph and took the banjo out of his hand. "I let you out of my sight for five minutes and the boy comes home thinkin' he can be a waiter. What are you thinking of? Wanderer, with all his brains, all his book learnin'. He will be a teacher. That's what he will be."

Randolph folded his arms in front of him. "The boy should be whatever he wants to be. And a waiter at The Rennert is more respected than any old, shabby, eyeglass-wearin' teacher. And makes more money too. You've seen them. They are the top, and they know it. To be a waiter at The Rennert. You're not goin' to top that. You jes' let the boy talk. He's not doin' anything but talkin' anyway.

"We was havin' a nice day. Now you get all on your high horse. You're not Miss Helen. Stop acting like her."

Arbutus turned away. "Mama, are you hearin' this? Can you believe what this boy is sayin'? A waiter?"

Myrtle opened her eyes, rocked a few times before she responded. "'Butus, there ain't nothin' finer than workin' at The Rennert."

January 2, 1915

Hollins Street

Helen made sure she was downstairs early enough to make her phone call before Myrtle came to fix breakfast. She was sure that Stroemeyer would be in. She was less sure that he would answer his phone. She gave the number to the operator, then replaced the earpiece after ten rings.

To pass the time she sat at the dining room table, pulled the folded sheet from her skirt pocket and reviewed it. Yes, she said to herself, this is the right thing to do. A good decision, a good way to start the year.

She called to Myrtle as she heard the click of the lock in the back room. "Happy New Year to you. I hope you had a nice day with your family. I could smell that wonderful holiday aroma yesterday afternoon when I stepped out on the back porch. Good to have family around, isn't it?" She was unaware of the irony of her words.

Myrtle unbuttoned her coat and hung it on the familiar black iron hook. She turned to Helen, but before she could ask for her breakfast order, Helen told her that she desired privacy for a call she must make. Myrtle nodded and headed for the kitchen steps. "Jes' call when you're ready. I'll be right here fixin' it up."

Helen returned to the phone and this time reached Stroemeyer's secretary, who put Helen directly through to his office. They made plans for him to come to Hollins Street late the following afternoon.

The next day, he sat with his client whose family had been with the firm since its founding. He listened while she read from the paper she had prepared. When she finished, she folded her hands and placed them in her lap.

Stroemeyer paused before he spoke. "Mrs. Aylesforth, are you sure that this is what you want to do? Have you given this change sufficient thought?" His voice was soft, gentle, but he was also aware of the potential for trouble when the time came to execute this plan.

"Raymond, I do appreciate your concern, but I assure you that I have given this much thought. I am aware that my funds are rather limited, but then my time is rather limited as well. The house and its furnishings will go to Cantata. They are comfortably fixed enough that any money that I might leave her would not impact her living standard. The proceeds from the house should be more than enough to satisfy any hunger there.

"So, yes, this is what I want to do. This bit of money will mean a great deal to those who receive it. And I must be sure that Myrtle is taken care of in the years that she has left." Helen stood, and Stroemeyer recognized that the meeting was over.

He stood, folded his notes and placed them in his jacket pocket. "I will send my secretary around on Friday with the papers for you to sign."

Helen hesitated. "Raymond, I would prefer it if you could bring them by. I would like to keep this between the two of us. For the time being, of course."

Stroemeyer smiled. "I will call you and we can arrange a time for that." He turned to leave, then stopped. "Mrs. Aylesforth, may I ask if you are planning to tell your family about this change?"

Helen stood by the door. "No, you may not ask," she answered, with a smile that softened her words.

March 8, 1915

Hollins Street

That afternoon Myrtle noticed her daughter as she approached the back door. "Good that you're home early. Good that you are here. I think it will do Miss Helen good to see you, talk to you. She needs some cheerin', I think. Spends too much time here, alone, all this quiet. Too many books."

Arbutus kissed her mother and went to the front room. Helen sat in the chair in the bay window, book in her lap, unread. She turned when she heard someone enter, tried to smile when she saw who it was. "Come here and let me look at you. All dressed up in this new fashion."

Arbutus came to the center of the room and twirled around, the kelly-green plaid poplin of her top, which she had chosen to accentuate her eyes, turning with her. The hobble skirt, a black serge, made her steps stilted, and she bobbled purposely.

"And look at my petticoat." Arbutus lifted her skirt to show a fine ivory silk, falling in two tiers, each banded with a plaid ribbon that matched the dress. "No one will see that it matches, but I know it does. I make petticoats for my clients too, to match their outfits, whether they can be seen or not. Somethin'," Arbutus corrected herself, "something special. And, my customers, my clients, they think it's special too."

Helen smiled to hear the authority in the younger woman's voice. She nodded. "It suits you, those straight lines. It's important that your customers see you as a model of fashion, not simply as a dressmaker. You are definitely making sure that they know that you are not just a dressmaker."

Arbutus allowed herself to grin, pleased to hear the familiar sternness in her benefactor's voice. "I think they know that I'm not just a dress-maker." She turned again, making sure that her skirt was in place.

"And I'm here to make sure that you're fashionable too. It has been so long since I've made anything for you. So, for this spring, you will have three new outfits!"

Helen touched the seat beside her, indicated that Arbutus should sit. "Now you know that I am not my daughter. So three outfits is out of the question. But one, well, I wouldn't say no to one." Helen looked Arbutus over. She is looking fine, she thought, just as she should. Capable, confident. That will help her business. "You choose the style, the materials, the colors, Arbutus. Just be sure that the finished product is something appropriate to my age."

Arbutus smiled. Miss Helen and her soberness. No wonder people are scared of her, she thought, and folded her hands in her lap.

Taking a deep breath, she said, "But I do have something else to talk to you about." She made sure that her back was straight. Miss Helen will notice that, she thought.

"I have been keeping records, of expenses, of payments. Lillian Gish has actually been helping me with these. She has a gift for numbers.

"And we are doing fine. Of course, the rent has been paid in advance, so we have had that extra money for these past months." Arbutus inhaled, tried to keep her heart from beating so quickly.

"So, what I am here to discuss, to ask you about, is." She stopped, tried to remember the words she had rehearsed. "We, Randolph and I, want this business to be mine, ours. We want to have it on our own. Now I know that some of the money you used to help us was due to Randolph, though Mama wouldn't let us take it. And you used that. So, that is good. If you could tell us how much, that would help us know better about money, what it cost to put it together, the business, I mean. And, if you put any of your personal money into it, we would like to make arrangements to pay you back. So that we can know that this business is truly ours."

Arbutus watched Helen's face carefully, trying to read her reaction. She hurried on. "It isn't that we don't appreciate all that you have done for us, Miss Helen. We could never repay that. But we do want to try to do this on our own. My own business." Arbutus licked her lips, swallowed, aware of the dryness in her mouth.

Helen put her hand to her forehead, rubbed her temples. Facing Arbutus, she said, "I do understand. And I have records of the moneys we used to set things up. Most of it would have been Randolph's, so you have no worries there. The few incidentals, let that be my small gift to you. It would give me pleasure, Arbutus." She walked to the sofa. 'Your understanding of this, your offering to repay any advance shows your character, Arbutus. You and Randolph. That character will stand you in good stead. Myrtle should be proud. I'm sure she is proud."

Helen took Arbutus's hand, held it briefly, then moved to the window.

Arbutus stood to leave, saw her mother's employer as she stood in profile. "Miss Helen, let me alter some of your skirts for you. I hope you won't think me out of line to say that you have lost weight. I can just take in the waist. It won't take me but a minute, and they will fit, hang better, much more comfortable for you." Arbutus flushed. "I hope you don't think me forward."

Helen, who did think it forward of Arbutus to speak of her appearance, was silent. Finally, she spoke. "That might be a good idea. Perhaps you can spare a few minutes this weekend. And we can talk about that new spring outfit you're making for me."

June 2, 1915

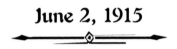

Eutaw Street

Arbutus turned the fan toward her and lay back on the sofa. The summer heat wave was in its fourth day. Temperatures over 100 degrees that fans could not mitigate. Wisely, her customers were staying home.

She had hoped to use the days to catch up, even get ahead on some of her orders, but the heavy fabrics for fall and winter, woolens, fur trim, satins, made the space seem more sweltering. When she attempted some of the hand sewing, perspiration from her hands dripped onto the fabric; the fine needles slipped from her hands.

Frustrated, hot, tired, she went to the sofa, unbuttoned the top of her cotton dress, pulled the chemise away from her wet torso, and cried. Glad that she was alone, that no one would witness her display of weakness, she fell asleep in a miasma of heat.

She woke an hour later, head and body aching. Pulling herself to her feet, she walked to the sideboard and poured herself some water. Almost as warm as the room, she thought as she drank it.

But mind-over-matter, she decided, and walked to the desk. Mind-over-matter. Where have I heard that? Miss Helen? Mama? Well, if Mama said it, it had to come from Miss Helen. She gathered scraps of paper together to begin to make sense of them. Invoices, notes on designs, schedules were heaped together. I must do better than this. I must make sure that all are sorted, arranged, before I leave each evening. Lillian Gish can help with the bills, but I must keep things sorted. This is a business, my business. I must rise to the occasion.

Arbutus arranged the papers, placed them in the manila folders she had purchased at the stationers. Rise to the occasion, she said to herself. And heard Helen Aylesforth's voice.

She lay her head down on the desk. "I don't know if I can." She was surprised that she had said these words aloud, and wondered how she had come to be in this pickle. She abruptly raised her head, gathered the folder marked "Invoices," and stood up. She realized that her dress was open, lay the folder down and stood in front of the fan while she fixed her bodice. Standing in front of the mirror, she repined her hair above her neck, stuffed the folder into her carpetbag, turned off fan and lights, and headed down the narrow stairway.

Enough for one day, she thought. Enough. She took no sewing with her that afternoon, and splurged on a cab to take her home. Randolph would be at work, the children would be at school, Myrtle would be at the big house. Only Melie would be there. Arbutus thought that she would have a few hours almost to herself. She closed her eyes, a slight smile on her face.

Twenty minutes later, as she walked down the alley, she saw that Melie was sitting in the back yard. In all this heat, Arbutus thought, but was grateful that she might have some time alone, if only for a few minutes. But when she opened the door, she saw Randolph sitting at the table.

"What are you doing home? What's wrong?"

Randolph looked up, and Arbutus saw a hardness in his eyes. "Well, I could say the same for you. Why are you not hard at work at your business?"

Arbutus heard him spit out this last word with bitterness and knew that he had been drinking. She walked to the table, and as she pushed his hand aside the pint bottle of Pikesville Rye skittered to the floor. The smell of whiskey filled the house. She bent down to wipe it up.

"That's right, woman, you better clean it up. That's what you're good for, cleanin'. You and your business. You're only good for cleanin'."

Arbutus stood up. "You get yourself right before the children get home, before Mama comes back. You get yourself up on those crutches and get out in the air." She walked around the room waving a dishtowel. "Why are you home now? What about your job? What have you done?" She heard herself screaming. "You can't let the children see you like this. Mama. Get yourself out in the air. Walk around. Come back not smelling like a drunk." She sobbed as she tried to get the words out.

Randolph reached for his crutches and struggled up from the chair. He lurched against the table as he rose and Arbutus ran over to help him. Still sobbing, she shouted, "Get yourself right. Please, Randolph."

He pulled away from her and walked to the door. "I can do for myself. I don't need you. You with your 'business'." And he walked to the alley.

Arbutus scoured the house looking for bottles. The one she found she tucked into her carpetbag. No more whiskey, she thought. He will do better just with the laudanum and cocaine. After all, those were recommended by the doctor.

July 30, 1915

Hollins Street

Abbott pulled to a stop in front of the house at precisely 5:15 p.m. Lillian Gish was waiting in the vestibule, wearing a white dotted-swiss dress tied with a yellow polka-dotted sash. Helen sat in the chair at the window. She did not rise when she saw the cab.

"Miss Helen would like you to come in," Lillian Gish called, and as he left the cab, John Abbott wondered what new assignment she would have for him. Always expecting something more, he thought.

As he entered, he was surprised at how small Helen appeared. Not only her size, but it seemed that she had lost some of her authority. She rose to greet him.

"Mr. Abbott, I seem to be a bit under the weather this afternoon. I would appreciate it if you would accompany Lillian when she sees Dr. Gatch." She returned to her chair. She had assumed that Abbott would assent, which, of course, he did.

He and Lillian Gish walked to the cab. "Can I sit with you in the front?" she asked. Abbott nodded. It was the first time she had spoken to him, and she smiled as he closed the door behind her.

August 4, 1915

Cablegram

August 4, 1915
London, England
To: Nicholas Sherwood
        Chesapeake Casualty Insurance
        St. Paul Place
        Baltimore, Maryland
        USA

Returning via SS Arabic leaving England August 19. Situation difficult here, but imperative to return. Mother not well. Please insure that house is ready to receive us.
Carry on.

Father

St. Paul Place

Nicholas asked Violet Marsh to call the staff together. They saw his smile while they gathered in his office, and anticipated his news. Everyone knew of the arrival of the cablegram. They applauded at his announcement, those who knew relieved that things would soon be back to normal.

August 20, 1915

Calvert Street

Cantata joined Nicholas at the breakfast table. He had the newspaper spread before him. "Russians, Germans, English, all in a mess." He folded the paper as Trude served breakfast. He nodded perfunctorily as she placed the plates before him. Looking at Cantata, he continued. "And it looks like Wilson wants us to get into the war. No good will come of that. We need to stick to our business here. Let them fight it out themselves. They didn't ask us; we need to stay out of it." He picked up his fork and started to eat.

"You made a good choice with Trude. Good cook, and quiet. The best combination."

Cantata reached for the toast. Buttering her slice, she said, "I plan to contact Zenobia this week, today actually. She's been checking on Father Sherwood's house every week, but it needs to be brought back into a livable condition.

"You've been sending her a remittance, haven't you? So make sure to send enough so that she can stock the house with enough food and necessities so that Mother Sherwood doesn't have to worry about that. I wonder how she is? Father's telegram was troubling; don't you think so?"

Nicholas nodded. "They've had a horrible experience. I can only trust that, once they arrive home, we can get back to normal." He looked over at his wife. "And you have been so good about overseeing things at Park Avenue. I know they'll appreciate it."

Taking a last gulp of coffee, he stood, kissed the top of his wife's head, and headed to the back door. He would drive to the office this day. He

2222

111111

11111

111

Cynthia Strauff

knew the day would be sweltering and wanted to avoid the long walk back with the afternoon sun blistering the concrete sidewalks.

He called over his shoulder, "Tell the children I'll see them this evening."

★★★

St. Paul Place

The cablegram was waiting on Nicholas's desk when he arrived that morning. News from Father, he thought, and looked forward to opening it.

Cablegram

August 20, 1915
London, England

To: Nicholas Sherwood
        Chesapeake Casualty Insurance
        St. Paul Place
        Baltimore, Maryland
        USA

We regret to inform you that Mr. Charles Sherwood and Mrs. Alice Sherwood were among those lost in the act of war on the part of Germany in the torpedoing of the SS Arabic on August 19, 1915.
The bodies have been recovered. Please respond with your wishes about disposition of remains.
Our sincere condolences.

James M. Middleford
President
White Star Lines

1

September 19, 1915

Hollins Street, The Alley

Wanderer came out of the bedroom; Myrtle stood at the stove, sausages sizzling. Melie was laying out the table. Arbutus and Randolph sat on their bed, sharing the *Baltimore Sunday Sun* between them.

Myrtle looked up at her grandson. "You get enough sleep, boy? That was mightly late you came in last night."

Wanderer stood in the middle of the room. "I am going to make you all happy this morning," he announced. "Good news for us." Making sure that all eyes were upon him, he continued. "They said that I am now an official busboy. Out of training. And I can start working, for money, next week. So that is my first step in becoming a waiter there." He looked over at his mother who had laid the paper aside and was standing up.

"Now, Mama, don't be worried. They know that I'm going to school. And my shifts are nights and weekends. And only one or two week nights, and my time doesn't start until dinner time, so I will have time to study." He noticed that his mother's frown hadn't changed.

"And it is just a job while I'm in school. So this gives me an alternative." He grinned as he used what his grandmother called a "fifty-cent word."

Arbutus smiled in spite of herself. "And you better keep thinkin' that it's an alternative," she answered, and drew out her last word.

That Wanderer, she thought. He can charm the dew off the honeysuckle. And then she worried for him.

PART IV
New Year's Eve, 1915

---◇---

Calvert Street

Nicholas was relieved that the house was quiet when he entered the back door. He did not call out; he wanted some time to himself, a few minutes of quiet. He turned left into the enclosed porch, chose the soft chair by the window. He fingered the Boston fern that hung in the window, brought from the Park Avenue house a few months ago. It seemed to be thriving, he thought. Would that I were faring as well.

Remembering the meeting at his office a few hours ago, he wondered if he had done the right thing, keeping the tradition of calling the staff together each New Year's Eve, one started the year his father had founded the firm. They expected it, and until last year, had always been rewarded with a bonus, some years more generous than others, and a few hours off to celebrate the holiday. This year the staff was smaller. Miss Marsh now handled switchboard as well as secretarial duties. She was a loyal minion, Nicholas thought. Someone who kept her opinions, her knowledge of how it had been, to herself. Johnston had let his assistants go, one in September, the other in early December.

Nicholas rested his elbows on his knees and put his head in his hands. Not a bit of new business, he thought, and that is my fault. I don't know what I'm doing and have no one to ask. For the past six months, no new revenues received, and February will see the three clients who paid their fees over twelve months ending their contracts. So it is get new business and get it quick, or close the firm.

He cringed at the thought of his father learning this, having to admit to him that he had failed. And then Nicholas realized that this would not happen. The reality of his father's death had left him, for just that second. On this last day of the year, he thought, I must admit to myself that I am not a success, that I am a failure, a disappointment in the eyes of my wife, my children, my friends.

Too much to bear, he thought, and tears came, unbidden.

He sat with his thoughts, his eyes closed, opening them when he sensed someone in the room. Cantata stood in the doorway, watching. She went to him when he lifted his head.

"Holiday times are sad when we think of those we love who are no longer here." She touched his shoulder, then sat on the sofa to his left. "It's just us tonight. A relief. No parties to go to. We can be here, just us. And I'll wear one of the mauve outfits that Arbutus made for the bereavement. It hasn't been six months, but no black tonight. I think the mauve will do just fine.

"Trude will feed the children early and take them upstairs after dinner. And I asked her to make us something special – whatever she would choose for a special dinner. So I think that it is going to be something German. And I want you to compliment her and encourage her. Don't dare say anything mean about Germany. She has enough to deal with from the other maids in the neighborhood. And Meg didn't treat her very nicely. I was surprised at that. So maybe it was a good thing that she found another job. Working in a chocolate factory. And Wockenfuss? Isn't that German?"

Cantata realized that her husband wasn't listening. "Oh, I'm rambling." She looked over at him. "Would you like to be alone for a little while? I can go up and dress, have Trude feed the children in the kitchen. That would give you some more quiet. We can be together later. And have some champagne. I think it would be all right for us to have some champagne, don't you? Even though we're in mourning. I think Father Sherwood would have wanted us to celebrate his memory, and hail the new year."

Nicholas had not yet looked up. Cantata rose, patted his hand. "You just sit for a while. Come upstairs when you feel better. I'll be dressing."

Nicholas grabbed her hand, kissed it, but said nothing.

Later that evening, the two sat at the dining room table, Cantata in her dress of mauve satin with a narrow lace trim at the sleeves. She wore the pearls that had been her mother's, given to her when she married

Nicholas, who wore a dinner jacket, his shirt fastened with pearl studs, and a diamond stick pin that had been given to him by his father on his 21st birthday.

"It's fine to be quiet this evening, Nicholas, to reflect on this year. So much sadness for you, for us."

Nicholas nodded, but said nothing.

"Terrible that this war is still going on. And tragic that there was no way to bring your mother and father back to their own country. How lucky – is that the word? – that Susannah is in England, that they are laid to rest there, with her, so that she can tend to their graves, see that they're not forgotten."

Nicholas looked at his wife. "Can we not talk this evening?"

Cantata suppressed a slight gasp, and picked up her fork.

Nicholas rested his elbow on the table, placed his hand by his mouth. "Oh, Cantata, I don't know what made me say that. Here you are trying to make the best of a sad celebration. Let's do have that champagne, and drink to the memories of Mother and Father.

"It all seems so dreamlike, inexplicable. A last trip to Germany, they thought." He smiled. "Well, it certainly was a last trip, wasn't it?

"Then the war, and it was as if they had disappeared. All those months with no word from them, no way to reach them. Trying to run the business with no direction. Seeing the business fall off. Then thinking they were coming home, that everything would work out. So happy, for just a few days."

Cantata watched her husband, noticed the tremor in his voice as he spoke.

"The nightmare of the burials, trying to reach Susannah, making arrangements with White Star, telling the staff, the children. It's all been too much, too much for me." Nicholas put his hand to his head.

"I'm not strong, Cantata. I wanted to be, but I realize that I'm not. It's just too much. It's all too much."

Nicholas realized that the words were pouring from his mouth. Cantata's eyes widened.

"The business, Cantata. There is no business, or there won't be in a few months. There is no money coming in. I've been draining the reserves for months, just to make payroll, even with the people that we've let go. By Spring it will be gone. Everything." Nicholas's voice broke with this last word. "I don't know what to do. I don't know who to go to. We'll be ruined. Everything my father built will be gone."

Working to regain his composure, Nicholas picked up the linen napkin, folded it into a neat rectangle, then refolded it into a square. He cleared his throat, replaced the napkin in his lap, then cleared his throat again. Cantata had not yet spoken.

"I'm so sorry to bring this to you, to tell you in this way." He looked to the far end of the table, his eyes not meeting hers.

"I spoke in an undisciplined manner. I didn't intend to frighten you. I'll think of something. I do have some time, a month, perhaps a bit longer. There is no need for you to be alarmed."

Cantata moved her chair closer to her husband, put her hand on the table. "Nicholas, I am your wife. You don't have to worry that I'm alarmed. I'm not a child; I'm your wife. And I want to be beside you through this. You don't have to solve this. We can solve it.

"You think that I'm concerned only with the house. But I have ideas. I can come up with ideas. I read the papers; I try to keep up, to think about what is going on in the world. We can get through this. We will get through this."

She picked up her glass, leaned toward him. "Let's finish our champagne. I'll stack the plates on the sideboard. Then we'll say goodnight to the children. An early night, this New Year's Eve. So we can face 1916 rested, together."

Cantata was sitting up in bed as Nicholas entered the bedroom. As he untied the sash of his navy woolen robe, she reached for him.

"I've been thinking about what you said earlier, Nicholas. There must be other companies that are suffering because of the war. Perhaps you could meet with them, see what they think. It's no use pretending that all is fine when you all know that it is not. I'm sure you're not alone in this predicament.

"And we have the Park Avenue house. We could sell it, or we could move there and sell this house, whichever you think would be better. That would give us some extra money, until you get on your feet again, until we get on our feet again."

Nicholas touched her hair. "You're willing to give up this house?"

"It's just a house, Nicholas. And, anyway, a Park Avenue address, well, that would be fine. You're a smart man, Nicholas. Even if the business has to close, people will be clamoring for you to work for, work with, them. Or you can open another business, on your own."

"I wish I had your confidence in me. But I don't think it will be easy. Father's will left everything except the house to Susannah. It looks like we are getting the better part of that arrangement, though I think Father would have never imagined it."

"And he left the business to you. Don't forget that."

Nicholas looked at his wife, but did not respond. "Yes," he said, "to sell one of the houses. Park Avenue would most likely fetch a higher price. We still have the mortgage here." His voice cracked as he anticipated saying farewell to the house of his childhood.

"But maybe it would be better for us to move there. Such a lovely street," Cantata said, and wondered which address would impress her friends more.

"Enough," she said, pulling back the blanket on Nicholas's side of the bed, "enough talk for tonight."

★★★

Hollins Street, The Alley

The family gathered in the kitchen, all awaiting Arbutus's return. She had promised to close the shop by early afternoon, said that she had only one client who had promised to be there no later than noon for a final fitting for a dress she planned to wear that evening.

Collards, these from Lexington Market rather than the ordinary Hollins Street Market, washed, and washed again, bubbled on the stove, next to the pot of black-eye peas, in anticipation of the next day's feast. Myrtle stood sentinel, holding two wooden spoons, one in each hand.

Randolph sat at the table, looking over at his banjo. He'd head out by himself this night, and was sad that there would be no Wanderer to accompany him.

Wanderer, dressed in black pants, long-sleeved white shirt, and black bow-tie, paced between the rooms, anxious to be on his way.

"Now you know, your mother said that you could not leave until she arrived, so no use wearin' out the floor." His grandmother looked at him sternly, then smiled, proud that he looked like a gentleman.

"Oh, Gramam, this is some night. They're lettin' me bus a private party. Only one other boy will be with me. And big tips. They say that there are big tips on holidays. And this one, all that drinkin', there should be some really big tips."

"Well, you be careful there. Stay out of the way, especially with all that drinkin' goin' on. Dangerous when men drink too much." She looked over at Randolph, who concentrated on adjusting the skin of the banjo.

Before Wanderer could respond, the door opened and Arbutus came in, arms full of packages. "Some candies, some cakes, from the market. They were getting ready to close out, almost gave these away. We can have some tonight, but save the fancy cakes for tomorrow."

She noticed Wanderer. "Oh, my big man. You do look a handsome one today." She laid her packages on the table, and went to her son, placed her hands on his shoulders. "Now you be careful tonight. Watch what you do. Watch those men, stay out of the way. And see if you can get someone to walk home with you, or at least part of the way." She stopped and reached into her carpetbag. "No. Don't walk home. Here. Take this. You take a cab. That is my New Year's gift to you."

Wanderer took the coins and put them into his pocket. "Now if I make so much money in tips, I can give this right back to you. And you'll see that you worry for nothing."

He pulled his coat from the hook. All eyes were on him.

"I'm off. This night will be an adventure. I'll see you in 1916!"

★★★

The Rennert Hotel
Liberty and Saratoga Streets

Wanderer watched the couples as they entered, and wondered how many women were wearing dresses that his mother had sewn. He smiled to himself, thinking that he had this secret knowledge.

He was one of two busboys assigned to the party, both following the directions of the four waiters who indicated what was to be done moving their fingers inside pristine white gloved hands. Like a ballet, Wanderer thought, or what he imaged a ballet to be. He resolved to learn about them, one of his resolutions for the new year.

Watching as the waiters refilled champagne flutes, their facile movements orchestrated so that glasses were topped off without the guests even being aware of it, he imitated their way of seeming invisibile as he cleared plates, glasses.

He stationed himself against a wall, adjacent to a Sheraton sideboard decorated with museum-quality sterling silver. A quiet period, no one needing his service, Wanderer used the time to observe. Rich people, he thought, and remembered his mother's words. The air was filled with talk and laughter, louder, more raucous as the evening progressed.

He sensed before he saw a movement to his left. A tuxedoed man had risen from his chair, lurched toward the man seated directly across from him. Wanderer saw him toss his drink in the man's face.

Diners from other tables rushed to quell the disturbance. The man drew back his fist and knocked the second to the ground, who rose to his feet, grabbed his assailant and threw him against the wall.

Wanderer did not have a chance to move as he felt the man's body smash into his. He felt his head slam into the corner of the sideboard. As he slumped to the ground, blood seeped into the collar of his starched white shirt.

Two waiters ran to help him. The fight had ended as quickly as it began, the two adversaries now seated at different tables. As Wanderer tried to stand, a man he did not recognize came over to him. "Let us keep this between us," he said, as he pressed a dollar bill into Wanderer's hand.

A waiter led Wanderer to the kitchen, where a cook gave him some ice to apply to his temple. "You'll have yourself quite a goose egg tomorrow," he said. "I hope your eye doesn't swell shut."

"Oh, I'll be all right," Wanderer responded, eager to return to the party in time to collect his tips. He thought about finding a fresh shirt, but then decided that he might get bigger tips if his battle scars were more apparent.

He walked home that evening, hoping that the cold air would help the pain in his head. Odd, he thought, that his entire head felt like it was in a vice, that the pain wasn't just where he had been hit.

He felt in his pocket where his mother's taxi money remained. He whistled as he walked, and wished that he had brought his harmonica with him.

New Year's Day, 1916

Hollins Street, The Alley

Lillian Gish slipped on the ice as she raced to the back door of the big house. She pulled herself up and kept running. Once there, she banged on the glass with both fists.

"Miss Helen, let me in. Please. Help me."

Helen heard the commotion; she had been sitting in the front window, waiting for Randolph's visit. She tried to hurry, aware now that her steps could not be rushed. She reached the door and pulled it open.

Lillian Gish rushed in. "Oh, Miss Helen, you have to come. We can't wake Wanderer up. He won't wake up. Not even for Gramam."

Helen turned the child around and followed her down the steps. She did not take time to find her coat.

"What happened, child? Tell me what happened."

But Lillian Gish ran ahead of her, back to the house, not hearing, or not answering.

Helen felt the warmth of the house as she entered. Greens and ham hocks simmered on the stove; the family was gathered in the bedroom. Arbutus held Wanderer's body against hers. Myrtle stood at her side.

"Ain't no use, baby. He's gone. Jes' like that, God took him. Needs him for work in heaven most likely. No use moanin'. God's will."

Randolph stood in the doorway, silent, watching. Melie knelt by her bed, praying.

Helen held the doorway, trying to catch her breath, the beat of her heart so intense that she could feel it in her throat. When she thought she was calm enough to speak, she asked, "What happened? What happened?"

And her last words came out in so loud a scream that everyone turned toward her, frightened at behavior that they had never experienced from her before.

At first, no one spoke. Then Myrtle turned to her. "He came in last night, just fine. We wanted him to wake us up to tell us all about it. He showed us his tip money; he even had a dollar bill."

Helen interrupted her. "What is that mark on his forehead, his right temple? Was he hit? Did he say anything about that?"

Arbutus looked up. She pressed Wanderer's head against her breast. "Not a word. He was just so happy, all that money he made."

"Let me call a doctor. He will know what happened," Helen said.

Myrtle took Wanderer's hand. "Ain't no use callin' a doctor, Miss Helen. God knows best, and He's called Wanderer home."

And Helen, who thought that she was always part of this family, sensed her separateness, sensed that they wanted her to leave, sensed that they wanted to be alone with their grief.

After she had left, Arbutus turned to Randolph. "You caused this. You and your music."

★★★

Hollins Street

She concentrated on each step as she returned to the house. She heard moaning, far away it seemed, and a part of her registered that it must be Arbutus or Camelia that she heard, such low-pitched moans, yet she knew they came from a woman. Drawn out syllables, gruff bellows, an unearthly clamor. The noises followed her as she entered the back room. It was then that she realized that the cries were coming from her, and she opened her mouth wide to let the sounds become louder, moans transforming themselves into a scream, the low-registered tone rising to a high-pitched screech. She stood in the middle of the floor and howled, knowing, and not caring, that she sounded like an animal.

She held onto the back of the chair and raised her head, howling, moaning, screaming. And then his name.

"Wanderer, my boy. Wanderer. Wanderer."

She walked to the front of the house, to the stairs, and, hand-over-hand, pulled herself to the second floor. On the landing, she pulled off her dress, threw her shoes into her bedroom, and went to the room, the room that had not been changed, bed, books, maps, all remained in order.

Silent now, she walked to the bed, sat gingerly on the edge, smoothed out the navy-blue cotton spread, looked over at the train set that still sat on the desk, the Black Watch toy soldiers arranged just as they had stood all those years ago.

Jimmy, she thought, Jimmy, I thought I'd never recover from losing you. And now this. It is just too much for me. It is too much to bear.

She pulled the pillow to her, inhaled what she hoped to be Jimmy's smell, long past, and lay down on the bed, stroking the pillow until she slept.

The next morning, she woke in her own bed with no memory of how she got there, the events of the day before swimming to the fore before she was totally awake. She did not have to remember. Everything was there, waiting for her to come to consciousness. The dress she wore the day before lay in a heap by the door.

Something must be done, she thought. I must do something; I must make this right.

She bathed and dressed quickly and went to the first floor. She would make a list. When she entered the dining room, she heard Myrtle in the kitchen. She didn't call to her, but descended the stairs, quietly. Myrtle was preparing breakfast for her employer.

Helen went up to her, put her hand on her shoulder. "Myrtle, I certainly did not expect you this morning. You need to be with your family, be with them. Then we will figure out what to do next."

Myrtle turned, her face dry, but her eyes yellow from tears shed. "Oh, Miss Helen, I had to leave that house. They have that boy there. Dead in the house, still in his bed. I can't stay in a house with no dead person, even Wanderer. And 'Butus, she just sit with him, holdin' his hand, all night. She was still there when I left, hadn't moved the whole night.

"Randolph just sittin' at the table. Sometimes he goes out to the yard. I think he has whiskey there, I don't know. And Melie down on her knees the whole night. She fell asleep that way.

"You know, I seen death before, but I never thought it would touch

Wanderer. That boy, I thought that boy was blessed. Blessed us all. I thought he was blessed."

Helen took her hand and led her to the table. "Let's sit here for a minute. Cooking can wait. Let's just sit and think, think what we can do next, what we should do."

Myrtle turned from the stove and walked to the table. The two women sat; neither spoke; neither felt they had to.

Finally, Helen broke the silence. "First things first, Myrtle. We must see that the boy has a proper burial. I would like him to be buried with Jimmy and Dr. Aylesforth. Fitting, I think. Yes. Loudon Park Cemetery. I can see to all the arrangements. I would be happy to do that. Yes. That is a good idea."

Myrtle didn't respond. Helen took that as a yes. The two women sat together, neither meeting the other's eyes.

After a time, Myrtle spoke. "Miss Helen, Wanderer belongs with us, with Joshua. He be buried in Oella, with our people there, with Joshua to look after him."

Helen swallowed. "Of course, Myrtle. I didn't think." She took a deep breath. "How thoughtless of me. Of course."

She turned to go upstairs, to sit in the front room, to think. Family, she thought. Wanderer belongs to them. And she wondered what had caused him to die.

Three days later, Christopher Columbus Corporal was buried in the Mt. Gilboa A.M.E. Church cemetery, Oella, to the right of Joshua Amos.

April 19, 1916

Hollins Street, The Alley

Arbutus left for work early each morning, arriving home just as Myrtle put dinner on the table.

Randolph went to work most days. He didn't tell Arbutus when he walked past the factory, heading to the docks. He kept Wanderer's harmonica in his pants pocket, carried it with him all the time, slipped it beneath the mattress when he slept. The men at the cigar factory noticed that he didn't talk so much anymore, certainly didn't laugh, or sing. His supervisor had to return much of his work to him to be rewrapped.

John Abbot now regularly escorted Lillian Gish to her appointments with Dr. Gatch. She sat in the front of his cab, and, most times, talked to him without putting her hand in front of her mouth. She slept in Wanderer's bed. Arbutus had insisted upon it. "Don't be superstitious. A bed is a bed," she said. But Lillian Gish didn't believe that she meant it. Lillian Gish saw a curtain come down between her mother and the world.

Melie knitted; Myrtle went to the big house every day, grateful that there was less and less work to do. She spent most of her time there sitting at the kitchen table. Some days she thought of earlier times, happier times, busier times. She remembered bustling into the house in the mornings, looking after everything, arriving while the family was still upstairs getting ready for the day. The smooth running of the household was her responsibility; everyone trusted her to see to that, even Dr. James.

She smiled as she pictured herself hanging up her coat, throwing down the wicker basket she always carried and heading straight to the front room to open the shutters and pull back the curtains. Oft times she waved to the vendors as their horses trotted down the street pulling wagons full of produce for the market. Then downstairs to put on the kettle, switch on the furnace. Oh, she thought, they needed me then. They couldn't have managed without me.

The cooking, and the polishing, and the shopping. A good family. And Dr. James always took care of emptying the chamber pots. Myrtle smiled at the sight of him walking down the stairs, holding the porcelain bowls, one in each hand, in front of him. Yes. A good family, she thought.

And these days, Helen spent her hours in the chair by the window in the front room, surprised to find herself waiting to hear the rumble of the farmers' wagons. She had once been exasperated when they passed in front of her house, infuriated by horse droppings left in their wake. Now, the familiar clip-clop of the work horses reminded her of an earlier time, a happier season. Most days she sat with a book in her lap, unread, and returned to her bed early, often while it was still light outside. She didn't notice.

June 19, 1916

———————◇———————

Charles Street

Cantata, wearing a black linen suit that Arbutus had made for her the year before, stood with Nicholas in Raymond Stroemeyer's conference room. She was not surprised to see Arbutus there, but she was startled when John Abbott entered the room. What, she wondered, was her mother's driver doing there? She stroked the organdy ruffle on her blouse, then nervously rubbed her hand on her skirt.

Stroemeyer's secretary brought tea for the group, helped them settle at the table. Cantata took the chair to the right of the head of the table. Nicholas sat beside her. Arbutus, nervous that she had been summoned, and never before having been in a law office, walked toward the opposite end. The secretary discretely led her to a seat at the left, one down from the head. John Abbott, twisting his cap in his hands and feeling the sweat in his armpits, glanced at the secretary and took the seat to the left of Arbutus. He and Arbutus stood when Stroemeyer entered. The Sherwoods remained seated.

The lawyer indicated that those standing should sit; he remained standing.

"A sad occasion has brought us here. I was privileged to know Dr. and Mrs. Aylesforth for many years. They were both fine people, and they will be missed." He adjusted his pince-nez, cleared his throat.

"Now to the business at hand." He paused; he had given some thought to how to conduct this meeting, and had decided that the fewer words he said, the better. Opening the file containing Helen's will, he read:

"First, to my daughter Cantata, I leave my house on Hollins Street and all its possessions. She may dispose of it as is her wish.

"Second, I leave seventy percent of my financial assets to Arbutus Amos Corporal, with the proviso that Myrtle Amos be provided for until the end of her natural life on this earth. The remains can be used as Mrs. Corporal sees fit, although it is hoped that at least some of the proceeds be used for the education of her children.

"Third, I leave the remaining thirty percent of my financial assets to John Abbott, in appreciation for his untiring service and his friendship."

Stroemeyer placed the document on the table. "That is the extent of the Last Will and Testament of Helen Hopkins Aylesforth. Are there any questions?"

Cantata stared straight ahead, hoping that the pounding of her heart was not visible. Nicholas looked at his wife, but said nothing. Arbutus sat with her hands in her lap. Abbott, who thought he had been called in to drive Arbutus home, realized that his mouth was open and took pains to close it.

Stroemeyer looked at those assembled. "If there are no questions, let me review the procedures we will follow. Mrs. Sherwood, I will have the deed to the Hollins Street property delivered to you by the beginning of next week. Mrs. Corporal, our office should be able to send you an initial payment by that time as well, as will we send one to you, Mr. Abbott. It will be some months before final payments can be made. We must make sure that any outstanding items are handled before we close the estate.

"Again, are there any questions?" No one moved. Stroemeyer straightened his papers and said, "Thank you for your attendance." He nodded, signaling that the meeting had concluded.

Cantata turned to Nicholas and rose from the table. She was deciding what to say to Stroemeyer when he approached her, an ivory envelop in his hand. "Cantata, your mother asked that I give you this. I hope it will help you understand." As he moved to pat her shoulder, she stepped back.

"Thank you, Mr. Stroemeyer. We anticipate receiving the deed to my house soon." She reached for Nicholas's hand; the two left the room.

Arbutus and Abbott remained standing at the table. Stroemeyer returned to them. "There is not a lot of money in Mrs. Aylesforth's estate, but I believe that it will be enough to make a bit of a difference in your lives. She spoke highly of both of you.

"Please leave your information with my secretary as to the best way to reach you." He shook hands with both, and left the room.

Arbutus looked at Abbott. Neither spoke. Finally, Abbott said, "I thought they called me here to drive you home. How about if I do that?"

Arbutus smiled and they walked into the corridor to wait for the elevator. Cantata and Nicholas had already left the building.

★★★

Park Avenue

Nicholas held Cantata's arm as they walked to the car. "Don't worry, Cantata. We'll have enough."

"I just want to go home," she said, her manner stoic. She held her mother's letter in her left hand. "I don't know if I can bear to read this."

Ten minutes later Nicholas helped his wife from the car, held her arm as they entered the house that they now called theirs.

"I'll have Trude make us some tea. Do you want to go upstairs to our room? Let me be with you when you open it." He put his arm around Cantata's waist.

She nodded and went to the stairs. "If you would wait for the tea, and then bring it up. I won't open it until you come." She studied the handwriting on the envelop, and saw how like her own it was.

When the tea arrived, she and Nicholas sat on the edge of their bed while she read:

> Dear Cantata,
>
> This will be my last letter to you, and I know when you read it you will be in a state of distress about the provisions of my will. I want you to know that I did not make this decision lightly. I put much thought into it, into how my remaining assets would best benefit those to whom I felt close.
>
> I know that you believe that I do not love you, or at least

do not love you the way that I loved Jimmy. In a way that is true. I will not deny it. But, Cantata, I love you as best I can, though it seems that we could never find any common ground, any common interests. That was always there between me and Jimmy. Perhaps you found that bond with your father. I hope that this was the case.

So if I have let you down, please know that I regret it. I wish things had been different, though there is no use in wasting time with wishes.

You and Nicholas have a good life, a secure life. I assume that you will sell my home, the home that I was born in and lived in every year of my life. Well, everything ends, and so that will be transformed into money for you, so that should please you.

It is important to me that Myrtle be taken care of. She has been part of my life since I drew my first breath, and her family has been my family. Wanderer is a brilliant boy. It is good that he will have the opportunity to pursue his education. The other child is also bright.

As for Mr. Abbott, he has been someone I could always call on, always count on. He never complained. He never asked for anything extra. He is a hard-working man whom I think deserves a bit of indulgence.

So, Cantata, there you have it. I wish you a good life.

Your mother,

Helen Aylesforth

Cantata folded the letter, replaced it in its envelop. She turned to Nicholas. "I'll have to find a new dressmaker."

A few days later, Nicholas asked his wife if she would like to visit the Hollins Street house, to see it one more time, to choose anything that she would like to have from it.

"Not a thing," she answered. "Nothing. Nor do I have any desire to revisit. It's best a memory that will fade to nothing. And the sooner the better, as far as I'm concerned."

"Any of your mother's jewelry, perhaps? As a," Nicholas hesitated, trying to think of a word other than memory, "a remembrance of better times?"

"She didn't have that much jewelry. And it isn't to my taste. So no. Well, yes. Bring it. And I can decide what to do with it later." She paused. "And maybe Father's desk. Yes, that. And his pen. I remember him sitting at that desk, writing. His pen. And the desk. And the jewelry. That's all. That is enough." She turned away from her husband.

Nicholas considered going to her, then decided that it was best to leave her to her thoughts.

June 21, 1916

Eutaw Street

Nicholas had contacted Arbutus, asked if it would be convenient for them to meet at her shop. "I think it would be better for us to make arrangements between ourselves. Then you can inform your family as you deem best." Arbutus thought she knew why he wanted to see her.

They met in late afternoon, after her clients had concluded their business. Arbutus stood at the window, watched as he got out of his car. Some shiny black thing, she thought. Always shiny, always new. She pressed her lips together as she heard him ascend the stairs. No use being nervous, she said to herself. No use being mad. Nothing to be mad over, at least not for me. And she was grateful that she did not have to confront Cantata.

Nicholas held his straw hat in his hand, and took the seat that Arbutus indicated. He refused her offer of tea or water. "You have a lovely studio here, Arbutus. I can see that you have an eye for color and design."

Arbutus did not respond, but worked to attempt a smile. She almost succeeded.

"If I may come right to the point. You know that Mrs. Sherwood has inherited the house. Well, she has decided to sell it, as I presume you presumed." He shook his head. No need to be nervous here, he thought, and wondered why he was not thinking quite straight.

"So. And I know this will be difficult for you. But I need to tell you that, in order to sell the house, we must raze the structure on the alley."

Arbutus looked puzzled. She lifted her hand slightly as she spoke. "I don't understand. Why would you want to raise that house?"

Nicholas shook his head. "Oh, I'm so sorry. I misspoke. I meant that

150

we will have to demolish your house, Arbutus. I'm sorry to have had to tell you this. It is just that the building is so old, and it has not been kept up. I mean that as no criticism of you. Rather I am speaking from a structural standpoint, so that the property cannot be sold with your house as it is."

Arbutus looked up at the ceiling. Why had she not anticipated this? Of course, Cantata would sell the house. They would have to go, one way or another. This was just a quicker way of leaving.

"I do understand that this might have come as a surprise to you. Both Mrs. Sherwood and I want to give you sufficient time to find other arrangements." He hesitated, waited for Arbutus to speak. "Ah, if you could give me an idea of how long that would take, it would be helpful to us."

Arbutus laughed. "For me, Mr. Sherwood, I could leave today and never look back, never miss it. But Mama." She hesitated. "Well, that is not your concern." She stepped back. She needed room to breathe.

"Yes. Thank you for coming and letting me know. So that I will have time to tell my mother. I'm sure we can find another place to live without too much bother, or too much time. May I have a few days to let you know?"

Nicholas stood. "Take as much time as you need, Arbutus. Though we would like to be ready to proceed in two or three weeks."

"I'm sure that will be sufficient for us."

Nicholas rose to his feet. He shook Arbutus's hand. "Please know that my wife and I wish you and your family all the best."

"As does my family yours."

When she was once again alone in her shop, Arbutus straightened the pillow on the chair that Nicholas had occupied, picked up her carpetbag, and headed down the stairs. She locked the door with a firm turn, and headed north, toward Druid Hill Avenue.

June 23, 1916

It was still light when Arbutus opened the door. She had told Myrtle that she would be late, not to wait dinner, but her place was set, and Myrtle stood up to serve her meal.

"That can wait a bit, Mama," Arbutus said. "I have some news that we all need to hear." She looked at Randolph, and indicated that he should come to the table. She went to the bedroom door and called Lillian Gish and Melie.

"Let's all sit. I have important news."

When they had gathered, Arbutus spoke. She had rehearsed what she would say, and how she would say it.

"You know that Miss Cantata plans to sell the big house. Mr. Sherwood came to see me a few days ago to tell me that it would be put up for sale very soon." She looked to make sure that all eyes were on her. "Here is the situation. It is necessary for us to move." Without waiting for a response from anyone there, she continued. "So, I have found us a place, a whole house, three stories, on Druid Hill Avenue. And we can move in on the first day of July. We'll have enough bedrooms so that we can each have some privacy.

"Randolph, it is not more than an extra block for you to get to work. It is closer for me to get to the shop. Lillian Gish, it is about the same distance to your school. So, you see, this will be a much better place for us."

She looked around, waited for Randolph to congratulate her on finding a place. But no one spoke. Finally, Myrtle stood up. "Move? We gots to move? How can that be? I been livin' here, my family been livin' here for generations. This is the place where I was born. I ain't knowed nothin' else. How can you say we have to leave, 'Butus? How can you say that?"

"Mama, it will be better. You'll see. Big rooms, sunlight comin' in the windows. A house all your own, a yard all your own. It will be good for you. It's what Miss Helen would have wanted."

Myrtle faced her daughter. "You know, I lived through Mammy and Pappy leavin' this earth, I lived through Joshua dying, and my children, and even Wanderer and Miss Helen. And I got through it. I knowed that I could get through it. But I never thought I'd have to leave my home. Not my home. I never thought they'd take that from me." She walked out the door and stood in the yard, looking at the big house. She didn't utter a sound.

September 29, 1916

Druid Hill Avenue

Lillian Gish started running when, from a block away, she saw Melie on the front steps.

"What's wrong? Is it Papa?"

Melie was crying, trying to get the words out. "No. No, it's Mama. She left this morning for the market, and she hasn't come home. I don't know where she is. I don't know what to do. She's never been gone like this. I thought you'd never come home. I been standin' on the steps all this time, since noon time, waitin' for her."

Lillian Gish helped her aunt back into the house. "Let's sit for a minute, Melie, think where she might be." The young girl stroked her aunt's arm.

"Do you think she could have gone back to Hollins Street, to the alley? She hasn't said a word about it since we left. Do you think she went back? Did she say anything to you about doing that?"

Melie shook her head. "She hardly talks anymore. You know that, girl."

Lillian Gish stood up. "Let me go there and see if I can find her. Meantime you just wait here. I know that it will be all right. Try not to worry, Melie. Do you want me to get your Bible?"

Melie shrugged as Lillian Gish brought the book from her second floor room. "Here, you sit with this. I'll be back soon. I can walk there in less than half an hour. So don't worry. Promise me you won't worry?"

Melie stood, put her hands on her hips. "No more answers from no Bible. We have to figure out this life on our own."

Startled to hear these words from her beloved Melie, Lillian Gish giggled. She leaned over to kiss her aunt's forehead, then ran south, toward Hollins Street.

As she turned the corner into the alley, she saw Charlotte, Myrtle's friend, standing, facing the big house. She called to her, and as she ran, she saw Myrtle sitting on a tree stump.

"Oh, Gramam, we been so worried about you. Why didn't you tell anyone that you were coming here? One of us could have gone with you." She knelt in front of her grandmother.

"I jes' happened to be walkin' by and saw her. She was jes' standin'. Not doin' nothin'. Jes' standin'," Charlotte said. "She won't talk to me, but I know she knows who I am."

Myrtle looked at Lillian Gish. "It's gone. Everything is gone. No house, no nothin'. Everything I knew. It's just empty, like it never was. All my years I lived here, from a baby to havin' babies. It's like it never was. Even the lilac tree. Jes' like it never was neither."

Lillian Gish helped the old woman to stand. "I know, Gramam. That's why we didn't want you to come back alone. They tore down the house; I think they had to. And we knew it would hurt you to see it."

She looked up at Charlotte. "Thank you for staying with her. But I think we're fine to go home now." She stood. "And how are you doing, Charlotte?"

"Oh, everythin' changin'. You know how it is. We bein' pushed out by the Irish. So I don't know how much longer we'll be here either. You like it over where you are? Good colored people there, I hear. So maybe we can head that way. Or the children, at least. Me, I guess I'll stay where I am as long as they let me."

Myrtle stood quietly, her eyes on the place where her home once stood. Then grandmother and granddaughter, hand in hand, started the long walk home.

PART V
New Year's Eve, 1916

Park Avenue

Nicholas spent the day at home. In the early afternoon he walked north, wanting to see the houses that were being built along St. Paul Street, Calvert Street, Peabody Village they were calling it. So far away from the city, the area stretched from 25th Street all the way to 31st. The air was bracing and he wanted some time alone, to think, to plan.

The house on Calvert Street had sold quickly, though there was not that much cash after the mortgage had been cleared. Nicholas had concluded the sale of the business in late summer; its value lay mainly in the building it occupied, though both parties maintained the charade that it was more than that, announced that it was a merger rather than a sale, and Nicholas kept his title of Vice President, good enough for country club dinners and business club luncheons. The new owners viewed him as a steady sort who would cause no trouble. Nicolas kept his same office, but, as he was when his father was present, he remained unsure exactly what his duties were.

The sun was setting when he arrived back at the house. Cantata waited at the front window. She opened the door to him. "I was beginning to be concerned. So glad you're home now, in for the night." She wore the second of the mauve mourning outfits she had ordered from Arbutus the year before. "Here I am in mauve again. But we can say that this is a celebration, like we did last year. So much death, Nicholas. Though I think that I will end my official mourning tomorrow." She hesitated. "Well, perhaps not. People would talk. I guess they count mourning months like they do when a baby is expected." She sighed. "All this time, almost two years now, in black."

She stopped. "My, that does sound frivolous of me, doesn't it? Perhaps Mother was right."

Nicholas led her back to the front room. "Try not to think about her, not tonight. And you look lovely in black. And purple, by the way." He smiled, hoping to please his wife, and poured them each a small glass of sherry. The crystal decanter and glasses had been his father's, and he pictured his parents in this very room, years ago, celebrating New Year's Eve, Nicholas and his sister Susannah sipping grape juice, almost the same shade as their parent's wine.

He looked at Cantata. "Why don't we have the children dine with us this evening. Include them in on this celebration. They're old enough now. And I think they're old enough to start having dinner with us. So much extra work for Trude to prepare separate meals. They'll soon be grown, gone from us. I see so little of them. Let's do that? What do you say?"

Cantata, who preferred to have Nicholas to herself, hesitated. She sensed that this was important to her husband, who made so few suggestions, let alone demands.

"If you would like that, of course we can do it. I'll go up and tell them to dress for dinner, that this will be a special celebration. And you can be the one to tell them that they are now officially grown up enough to have dinner with us every evening. Would you tell Trude about the changes? I hope that she can manage to combine the two menus so that it works out for us."

Nicholas smiled, the first one that Cantata had seen in many months. "I'm sure it will be fine. It's not about the food, you know."

He stood to find Trude. "I have a feeling that the move to Park Avenue was good for us, is going to be good for us, all of us."

Cantata nodded, and walked up to the children's rooms on the third floor.

★★★

Ensor Street

John Abbott called out as he pushed the front door open with his knee. "Come help me, Anita. I brought things home for our celebration!"

His wife appeared from the kitchen, and grabbed the bag that was slipping from John's left hand. "Oh, you have been shopping, that German store on Eutaw Street. What did you buy?"

"Here's the best. Champagne tonight. Let's put it on top of the ice box. There's enough ice left up there to chill it." Abbott walked into the kitchen, bottle in hand. He opened the back door, and a brown and white, three-legged mongrel hopped in. "Come on in, Scout. You can celebrate with us." Abbott placed the bottle in the tin-lined compartment atop the wooden chest and walked into the living room. Scout followed and jumped into the chair before Abbott reached it.

"Get that dog down. His paws are still wet from the slush outside."

Abbott pulled his handkerchief from his pocket and wiped the dog's paws. "That better?"

Anita shook her head. "This is what comes from not having any children, John. We're both silly about that old mutt."

Later that evening, the two sat on the sofa, enjoying their first-ever taste of champagne.

"It's been quite a year, hasn't it?" John said. "All that money coming in, unexpected like it was."

"And sitting in the savings and loan, just waiting for us," Anita said. She leaned into her husband. "Have you thought any more about buying your own cab?"

"Sometimes when I'm driving, I think about it. But it seems like a lot of work. Would have to advertise, have a phone. Just too much work. This way, I drive when I want, and if I have enough money, then I can stay home. That sounds like a pretty good life to me. And now we have a nest egg; we won't have to worry about anything. It's good, just to have enough, don't you think."

Anita looked at him, raised the juice glass that they used for the champagne, and said, "I do."

***

Druid Hill Avenue

Randolph, his shift at the cigar factory over, was home before dark. He stood on the back porch and looked at the yard. Melie said that come spring, she'd help Myrtle plant a garden. So this is my domain, he thought. I am looking over my domain. But he knew exactly whose domain it was, though Arbutus never mentioned it. She didn't have to. And he thought back to a New Year's Eve, just a few years ago. A lifetime ago. The harmonica. Had that caused it all? Was Myrtle right? Had blaspheming the reverend brought God's wrath down upon him, upon them all? Well, no more music in this house. No more laughter either.

And here we are, living in the big house, he thought. Almost as big as Miss Helen's. But without Wanderer. Wanderer, who would have made it all fit together, who would have made us laugh, who would have made sure that there was music in the house.

He reached for the bottle in his pocket, unscrewed the cap, and drank the rest. That's one half-pint gone, he said to himself.

He turned when he heard someone behind him. "Come on in, Randolph. No use standing out here in the cold, thinking. Not good to think too much, you know that." It was Melie, talking now, talking more than he had heard her the whole time they lived on the alley. Randolph shook his head. No accountin' for the Lord, he thought, jes' no accountin'.

"Where'd you pick up all that sense, Melie. That been in your head all these years, jes' comin' out now?"

"I mighta been quiet, but I was watching, as best I could with these cloudy eyes, and I was thinkin'. Mr. Lawrence says I should talk more, let people know who I am. And so that's what I'm tryin' to do. How's it workin', do you think?"

"It's workin' jes' fine, Melie. And Lawrence, it's good he come into your life. Jes' like that. You got a beau, a suitor, I would say."

"Oh, yes. He come down the alley most every day, and he save the best produce for us. Mama says jes' like Pappy did when he was courtin' her.

"You're a good woman, Melie. But don't let nobody take advantage of you. Be on your guard."

"Randolph, I had all my life to be on guard, sitting in that house, that dark house, thinkin' that's all the life I was meant to have. Look at me now. Arbutus's movin' us here, well, not so good for Mama, but it be good for the rest of us, for you, if you let it.

"Arbutus love you, you knows that. She jes' need some time to get over Wanderer. Then it be good with you and her again. But you needs to stop drinkin'. That ain't never goin' do no good for nobody."

Randolph nodded, halfheartedly, more to get Melie to stop talking than in agreement.

Melie raised her head. "Smell that, Randolph? He's comin' down the street. Let's you and I go out and each get one. A baked sweet potato. Mama always said that a hot sweet potato could turn the blues into smiles."

Without speaking, the two went to the street where, as Melie had predicted, the vendor was pushing his cart, the potatoes roasting in the smoldering coals.

A few minutes later, Lillian Gish came downstairs from her third-floor bedroom, looked for her grandmother who was not at her usual place in the kitchen. Since they had left the alley house, since the day that Lillian Gish had found Myrtle back on Hollins Street, since Melie, with her own room and a house full of light, had come into her own, Myrtle had left more and more of the cooking and cleaning to her daughter and granddaughter. Myrtle had her own room as well; it looked out on the back yard. Some days she sat, looking out her window, imagining that she was in Miss Helen's big house, looking out on her home. Home was the last thing she thought about at night, and the first thing she thought of in the morning. Even before her eyes were open, she was imagining herself back home.

This place, she thought, with all its rooms, with all its light, its bathroom and water closet that the family raved over, it will never be home to me. But here I am and that house is gone. Gone, she thought. How could they have made my house disappear like that? No sense. Rich people have no sense.

Myrtle walked to the market, Lexington Market, a few times a week. But it was so big, so crowded, she hadn't made friends with any of the stall keepers. Nor had she made friends with any of the neighbors. Too high-falutin', she said, when Arbutus encouraged her to get outside, go up and see the neighbors. "They need to come to me. I ain't beggin' them for no talk."

Lillian Gish had the third floor to herself. She sweltered when it was hot; she shivered when it was cold; but it was hers. She felt freer, as if a door had opened for her, as if part of Wanderer, the smart part, had been passed on to her. Maybe it was because she slept in his bed, that bed had come with them from the alley to Druid Hill Avenue. And though she never said so, her heart ached to see her brother, who made her smile, who made her dance. She still didn't talk much, but she talked more. And once in a while she smiled without putting her hand in front of her mouth.

Randolph knew it was Arbutus when the front door opened, although she no longer called out that she was home, and she would especially not call out this evening, this New Year's Eve. He went to the vestibule, met her as she hung up her coat.

"We need to get through this night, get through tomorrow, baby. It'll be better then, for everyone. We can't just keep all this locked up inside. None of us."

She pushed him aside, although it was a gentle push. "Not now, Randolph. Just let me think, let me think." She went to the stairs to their bedroom that faced the street. She called to him. "You come, come with me. Just keep me company for a bit. Ask Lillian Gish to set the table before you come up. Tell her that we'll all eat together tonight."

E P I L O G
New Year's Eve 31, 1936

---◇---

Well, I told you that this was not my story, but I was part of it, a small part of it. And don't expect a "and they lived happily ever after" ending. This is life, not a fairy tale.

I guess you want to know how the story ends. But no story ever really ends, does it? We keep on living, or dying, and some days, some times, are good; some days, some times, are callous. But we go on, or at least most of us do.

So, I'll fill you in on what I know. This is not made up, that I promise you.

The Sherwoods still live on Park Avenue. Cantata, if you met her, would be charming and gracious. But she cries at night and never got over wanting her mother to love her. (Maybe I made that up.) Nicholas goes to work every day, always the gentleman. It's only when he goes to his back door and looks up at the stars that he acknowledges to himself that he is a failure. He loves his children, though, and, even though they're grown, to them he is the world.

I see John Abbott and his wife every few years. He still drives his cab, although they've been updated over the years. He thinks he will retire in a year or two. They want to buy a home on Back River and crab in the summertime. A few years ago, he and I visited Miss Helen's grave. I told him that if she were still alive, she'd have him owning, running, the biggest cab company in Baltimore. He laughed. He's a good man.

And now to my family. Well, Melie did marry Lawrence. You see, miracles do happen. They live a few blocks away, on McCullough Street, and he makes sure that our house still has the (second) best produce.

Papa never did stop his drinking, or the laudanum, or the cocaine. Somehow he kept his job, but he lost his gold tooth. He never did tell us about that, but we knew it wasn't a happy story. He never recovered from Wanderer's death, always felt responsible, and Mama never let him forget it. He came home one evening in

163

1918, lay down on the sofa and never got up again. Spanish flu. Gramam cared for him. Of course, she got it too, and she died two days before he did. So death visited our family again, but it was nothing like when Wanderer died. I guess you could say that we had been to Hell once, so anything else, well it just made us tougher.

How quickly it became just the two of us, Mama and me, in that big house. I kept my room on the third floor. I liked the privacy; I liked being alone. So did she. I went on to high school; there was never a question that I would not. And the spring that I was to graduate, Mama said that she would send me to college, anywhere I wanted to go. I chose Howard, close enough that I could come home and check on how she was doing. I was nervous leaving her alone, all on her own.

Her business prospered; she worked most all the time. Until the crash. And then the rich folk, who could never get enough, found that they had to make do. No more dresses, no more evening gowns. So Mama closed the shop. She found a job as a seamstress at Hutzler Brothers, and, as she says, was glad to get it.

But she kept the house. And that's where we live now, she and I.

Now, as for me, I came back to Baltimore and got a teaching job, not that I like children, nor do they particularly like me, I might add. But what else could I do? And at night, I write stories. Like this one.

Acknowledgments

In my research for this book, I happily stumbled on a volume that gives a brilliant perspective to the area and time. *Baltimore's Alley Houses*, by Mary Ellen Hayward, proved an invaluable resource. I recommend it to historians and sociologists everywhere, and anyone interested in the history of Baltimore.

To my husband, Dick Schaub, a delicious resource, thanks for spending hours driving, searching, and finally finding the Baltimore of the 1910s. A superb proofreader, map genius, and unflagging cheerleader, you made this process a romp.

And, of course, to my lovely Sasha, for phone calls and visits unparalleled.